BALLERINA DETECTIVE

and the Missing Jeweled Tiara

KAREN RITA RAUTENBERG

DNA Press™

©2009 DNA Press, LLC

Library of Congress Cataloging-in-Publication Data

Rautenberg, Karen Rita. Ballerina detective and the missing jeweled tiara / by Karen Rita Rautenberg. — 1st ed.
        p. cm.
Summary: Twelve-year-old Kayla uncovers a mystery while performing in the Nutcracker ballet, struggles with stage fright during a school play, and experiences her first crush on a boy.

ISBN 978-1-933255-47-7
        (alk. paper)

[1. Ballet dancing—Fiction. 2. Mystery and detective stories.] I. Title.
        PZ7.R195448Bal 2009
        [Fic]—dc22

        2 0 0 9 0 2 1 2 9 6

DNA Press, LLC
www.dnapress.com
editors@dnapress.com

Publisher: DNA Press, LLC
Executive Editor: Alexander Kuklin, Ph.D.
Art Direction: Alex Nartea
Cover Art: Studio-N-Vision (www.studionvision.com)

This book is devoted to Joan, Jennifer, Louis, Anthony, Matthew, Andrew and Alyssa.

"Once again, Karen brings you inside the world of a determined young girl
who through perseverance and brains endeavors to solve a mystery,
and takes her readers on a fun romp doing it."

Trish Marx, author of *Elephants and Golden Thrones,*
Inside China's Forbidden City and many other books for children.

Table of Contents

Chapter One

THE JEWELED TIARA

Kayla walked into her ballet school. She changed into her black leotard, pink tights and ballet shoes in a dressing booth. Then she walked over to her locker.

"Hi," said Vicky, opening up her locker next to Kayla's.

Amber came over to them. "Please come to my locker." They went over to her locker in the back of the room.

"Look at my tiara. It's real gold with genuine jewels on it. My mom wore it in a ballet," said Amber, holding it up.

The other girls came over to admire the tiara.

"Wow, the jewels are sparkling," said Cindy.

"Girls, what are you doing?" asked Madame Sofia, coming over to them.

"Could I use my tiara for the King of Mice's crown that Marie wears?" asked Amber, showing it to her.

"Of course, it's lovely," smiled Madame. "It's time to start class now."

The girls followed Madame into the studio. They took their places at the barre, a wood hand rail that goes around the walls. The three boys joined them.

Madame turned on slow music on the stereo. "Let's do our warm-up exercises now," she called out.

They did pliés and relevés holding onto the barre.

When they finished, Madame clapped her hands. "Come to the centre now."

"Guess what? Amber brought in her gold tiara with real jewels today. Madame said she can wear it in the Nutcracker," whispered Amy to Dylan and her brother Julien.

"Cool," said Dylan, "cuz I'm the prince who crowns her."

"Let's do arabesques," Madame said. The dancers stood on one leg and stretched the other leg out behind them.

"Next are pirouettes," called out Madame.

When the music got faster, Kayla started spinning too fast. *Uh-oh, I feel dizzy*, she thought, bumping into Nicole. They fell on the floor.

Nicole yelled. "You dance like an elephant."

"Ha, ha," laughed Megan.

Cindy and Shanté giggled.

"I I'm sorry," stammered Kayla, her face turning red.

"Let's practice leaping now," called out Madame.

The dancers started leaping across the floor, looking into the mirrored walls.

"Ouch," moaned Amber, falling on the shiny wood floor. "Someone tripped me."

Madame stopped the music and rushed over to her. "Are you alright?"

"My ankle hurts a little, but I'm okay," Amber said.

"Let's stop now," said Madame. The dancers sat down on the floor in front of her.

"When do we start practicing for the Nutcracker Ballet?" Amy asked.

"Now that it's September, we'll be starting our rehearsals in our studio next week. Last week, I hung up the casting list including the understudies from most of my classes on the wall in the waiting room. As you know, Amber has the star role as Marie. Her two understudies are Amy, who is also the Sugar Plum Fairy and Megan, who is also in the Dance of Hot Chocolate. Dylan is the Nutcracker. He turns into the prince and takes Marie to the Land of Sweets. Dylan's understudy is Connor."

"Madame," called out Cindy. "When are we going to have toe dancing lessons?"

"The girls will start in January," smiled Madame.

"Hooray," yelled the girls.

The girls curtsied and the boys bowed to Madame and they went to their dressing rooms.

"Megan, Shanté and Nicole were mean to laugh at you. You're a very good dancer," said Vicky, putting her curly brown hair in a ponytail with a hair band.

"Thank you. I've been taking ballet lessons for four years, and now I'm 12," said Kayla, combing her long, sandy blond hair.

"I started taking ballet lessons when I was seven years old when I lived in Ohio. Now I'm 12 1/2," Vicky said.

At that moment, they heard Amber screaming. All the girls raced over to her locker. "My tiara is missing," sobbed

3

Amber, tears rolling down her face.

Madame rushed over to Amber. "What happened?"

"My tiara is gone. Someone stole it," Amber cried.

"Oh, dear me, this is terrible. I will have to call the police and report this as a robbery," said Madame.

Amber nodded. "Alright."

"Where was it the last time you saw it?" asked Kayla.

"I left it in my ballet bag on the bench in front of my locker. I was in such a hurry, I forgot to put it in my locker. It's not in here anymore," cried Amber, holding up her pink ballet bag.

"This is horrible," Kayla said.

"Oh, Kayla, I remember you telling me you had a knack for solving mysteries. Could you please help me find my tiara?" pleaded Amber.

Kayla sighed. "Um, okay."

"I'll help her," added Vicky.

Madame raised her eyebrows. "That's nice of you girls but be careful." Then she left the room.

Amber's green eyes lit up. "Thank you. It's very valuable. I feel I need to wear my tiara for good luck."

"We'll do our best to find it," said Vicky.

"When all the girls leave, let's look for clues," whispered Kayla to Vicky. They changed into their shirts, jeans and sneakers in separate dressing booths.

Several minutes later they were standing in front of the locker with Amber's name on it. Vicky squatted down on her knees and looked under it. "Oh, I see a gold barrette," she said, picking it up. "Let's save it as a clue."

When they got back to their lockers, Kayla put the barrette into a small ziplock bag. They sat down on a wood bench.

"Who do you think the barrette belongs to?" Vicky asked.

Kayla shrugged. She took out a small notebook from her backpack. "Detectives should take notes," she said. She wrote down suspects and motives on a page in her book.

"Also write clues," said Vicky, taking a sip from her water bottle.

"Alright," said Kayla, biting into her red apple. On another page, Kayla wrote clues. Then underneath clues, she wrote gold hairclip.

"Who do you think stole the tiara? And also, who tripped Amber today?" asked Vicky.

Kayla shrugged. "It may be the same person. Whoever stole the tiara may have known that Amber doesn't have a lock on her locker."

"I think all the boys and girls took a break today. Anyone could have sneaked into the girls' dressing room. But I think the two main suspects are Amy and Megan. They're the two understudies for Marie," said Vicky.

"I'll write down Amy and Megan on the suspect list and their motives," said Kayla.

"Who else could be a suspect?" asked Vicky.

"Oh, now I remember. During class I overhead Amy tell

her brother Julien and Dylan that Amber brought the tiara in today," said Kayla.

"Julien is only a toy soldier, but he may want his sister, Amy, to get the star role," said Vicky.

"Dylan is the prince. He wants Amy to be Marie because he has a crush on her," said Kayla.

"Maybe Cindy did it. She really admires Amy. Also, Amy and Cindy often wear barrettes. The gold barrette could be one of theirs," said Vicky.

Kayla added Julien, Dylan and Cindy to the suspect list. "It's too bad Amber left her tiara on the bench," Kayla sighed.

"It made it much easier for someone to steal it," Vicky said.

"That's true," Kayla agreed.

"Oh no, it's almost 6:00. I have to go home now," said Vicky. They ran out the front door of the ballet school together.

"Bye," Kayla said.

"Bye," Vicky said. They walked in different directions.

Kayla's cell phone rang. "Hi Grandma. I'm sorry I'm late. I'm coming home now."

Kayla opened the front door of her white and green split level house on Long Island. Oliver, her gold, black and silver haired Yorkshire Terrier jumped up on her and followed her into the kitchen.

"Hi, honey," said her grandma, turning over the fried chicken in the pan on the stove.

Kayla's blue eyes lit up. "Hi, Grandma Millie."

"Please make us a big salad," said her grandma.

"Alright," said Kayla, and she started making the salad.

"Hello," said Kayla's mother, walking into the kitchen.

"Hello, Maggie," said Kayla's grandma to her daughter.

"Hi, Mom," said Kayla.

"Hello, honey," said Kayla's mom.

"Oh, Mom, you're wearing the cultured pearl necklace Dad bought you," said Kayla as they sat down at the dining room table.

Grandma sighed. "It's too bad that you and Dan are divorced now."

"Oh, Amber's tiara was stolen at ballet school. Vicky and I offered to try to find out who stole it and get it back," blurted out Kayla.

"It could be dangerous," said her mother, pushing her blond bangs out of her eyes.

"Don't worry Maggie," said Kayla's grandma. "Kayla can handle this. She's learned a lot from reading mystery books."

"Madame Sofia said that the girls in our class will soon be ready to start dancing on our toes. I don't know if I can do it," said Kayla.

"I'm sure you'll do fine. You've always dreamed of being a ballerina," said Kayla's mom, her blue eyes glowing.

Kayla shrugged. "I'm not sure what I want to be anymore."

"I've been reading manuscripts all day. It's hard work being an editor," said her mom, and she headed upstairs to her master bedroom.

Kayla cleared the dishes from the table and loaded them into the dishwasher. She heard her phone ringing and ran upstairs to her bedroom.

Kayla picked up the receiver. "Hi, Dad. Mom said I can spend my Thanksgiving vacation with you at East Highland."

"Great. Then you can meet my girlfriend Alyssa," said her father.

"Oh no, what about Mom?" asked Kayla.

"Your Mom and I already split up. I think you'll like Alyssa. Just give her a chance," said her dad.

"Oh, alright. I have to do my algebra homework now," said Kayla.

"You're good in math like me. That's why I'm an accountant. Anyhow, I'll call you soon. Bye," said her dad.

"Bye," Kayla said.

Chapter Two

A NEW PLAY IN DRAMA CLASS

Breanna, Marissa, Sarah and Kayla were walking to Island Hills Middle School together the next Monday morning.

"Hey, Halloween will be in a few weeks. Let's go trick-or-treating!" said Marissa.

"Aren't we too old?" asked Sarah.

"No," said Breanna.

"Our seventh-grade Halloween dance comes first," said Kayla.

"I know you want to dance with Jason," teased Breanna.

"And you want to dance with Tyrone," said Kayla.

"The dance should be fun!" said Sarah.

"Oh, by the way, Amber's real gold tiara was stolen at my ballet school. Vicky and I are looking for the thief," said Kayla.

"Wow, you're like real detectives," said Marissa.

"We're late. Let's hurry," said Sarah.

When they got to school, they rushed to their lockers and put away their jackets and backpacks.

Kayla made it to her drama class just before the bell rang. She sat at a desk next to Marissa.

Mr. Glasser stood in front of the room. "This year our

drama class will perform a new play called Princess and the Pirates. It's written by a friend of mine, Ray Jones. The show will take place in December. Auditions for the lead roles will take place in two weeks," he said, peering through his eye glasses.

"When do we get copies of the play?" asked Grace.

"You'll each get one today which you can keep," Mr. Glasser declared. "Crystal, please hand out the scripts."

Crystal gave one to each student.

Everyone started reading the scripts to themselves.

"I want a small part like a pirate," whispered Joe to Jamal.

"I'd love to be the princess, but I'm afraid to have such a big role," whispered Kayla to Marissa.

"I just would like to be one of the princess' girlfriends," said Marissa.

"I take acting lessons. I've had the star role in many plays," said Shannon loudly to her friends, Julie and Grace.

"She's always bragging," said Marissa to Kayla, frowning.

"Can we try out for more than one character?" asked Jamal.

"Yes," said Mr. Glasser.

"Maybe I'll try out for all of the parts," yelled out Jake.

"Yeah, Jake. You can even try out for Princess Emma," called out Zackery.

Everybody laughed.

"Good luck in practicing for your favorite parts," said Mr. Glasser at the end of class.

When the last bell rang at the end of the school day, the students headed for their lockers.

Sarah and Breanna came over to Marissa and Kayla as they got their jackets and backpacks from their lockers.

"Breanna and I are trying out for the seventh-grade basketball team. Do you want to try out, too?" Sarah asked.

"Oh, I'm a little too short," said Marissa.

Kayla rolled her eyes. "I can't get the ball into the basket."

"C'mon, try out anyway. You have nothing to lose," said Breanna.

Kayla and Marissa followed Breanna and Sarah into the girls' locker room. They changed into their white T-shirts and navy blue shorts.

When they walked into the gym, there was Ms. Taylor, the gym teacher and coach. She blew her whistle, tossing her black ponytail.

"Girls, we're going to start the tryouts now in order to see who makes the team. First, you'll practice dribbling the ball," said Ms. Taylor.

"Breanna, you really know how to dribble the ball fast," Marissa said.

"Next, line up at the foul line, so you each get to shoot fifteen foul shots," said Ms. Taylor.

Then the coach made the girls shoot the ball, ten times,

from different places on the court. Breanna made nine baskets, Sarah made seven baskets and Kayla and Marissa only made two baskets.

Ms. Taylor blew her whistle. "Tomorrow afternoon, I'll hang up a list of the players who made the team on the wall, outside of the gym. You all tried hard, but I can only pick the best eleven."

"I'm pretty sure I made the team. My older brother, Travis, taught me how to play basketball since I was six years old. He's on the high school team and hopes to get a scholarship to play in college," explained Breanna.

"I hope I made the team. My dad and I play basketball on the hoop hung up above our garage. He played basketball in high school," said Sarah.

The next afternoon in school, at the end of the day, Marissa and Kayla dashed to the gym.

Breanna and Sarah were already there. "Hi, girls! Sarah and I made the team," beamed Breanna, tossing her curly, black ponytail.

Kayla looked at the list. "Marissa and I didn't make it. Hey, look at the boys' posters. Tyrone and Anthony made the seventh-grade boys' basketball team," she said.

Sarah, Breanna, Marissa and Kayla waved good-bye to the security guard as they walked out the front door.

When Kayla reached her house, she walked into the living room. Oliver jumped up, licking her face. He followed Kayla into the kitchen.

"Hi," said her grandma, stirring the spaghetti sauce in a big pot on the stove.

"Grandma, the auditions for Princess and the Pirates are in two weeks. I doubt I'll get a big part," said Kayla. "I've only had small parts in my fourth, fifth and sixth grade plays. But I still want to be the princess."

"Then go for it. I think you'd make a good princess," said Grandma, pushing her short blond hair away from her face.

"Okay, I'll start reading the princess part now," said Kayla, and she ran upstairs to her bedroom.

Oliver bounded upstairs after her.

Chapter Three

SEARCHING FOR FINGERPRINTS

Finishing her homework the next night, Kayla turned on her computer in her bedroom. She went on Google and found many museums with spy exhibits and jewel collections. They were in New York and other states and even in France and England. Some of the museums had jewel robberies, like in the Netherlands.

Maybe I can go to one of the museums in New York, she thought, and printed out the articles.

Then she searched for detective stores in New York.

Oh, here's a store that sells detective things near my house, thought Kayla, and printed it out.

The following day after school, Kayla rode her red mountain bicycle to the shopping center near her house. She parked her bike and walked into the store that sold detective items.

A white-haired salesman came over. "May I help you?" he asked.

Kayla nodded. "Do you have a detective kit that can take fingerprints?" asked Kayla.

"We only have one kind of kit, but I'm sure it has everything you need," he said, handing it to her.

Kayla started to read all the items it had on the back. *There are so many things in it: two magnifying glasses, white fingerprint powder, a brush, fingerprint lifting tape, fingerprint specimen and file cards, a flashlight, plastic gloves. I can use all of these items. Hmm, there's also spy stuff. Code cards, wheels and tubes and rearview eye glasses. I doubt I'll need them*, she was thinking to herself.

"Would you like the kit?" asked the salesman.

"Yes, I'll take it," said Kayla, and she paid the cashier.

The next week, when ballet class was over, Vicky and Kayla went over to their lockers.

"Let's get fingerprints from Amber's locker and from the bench where her ballet bag with the tiara in it was. There must be some fingerprints left. Whoever stole the tiara may have looked in her locker before taking it from her ballet bag," Kayla said.

"How do we do it?" asked Vicky.

"I've got my detective kit with me. We also have to get fingerprints from the girls who are suspects before they leave. Just ask them to hold something, like a barrette," whispered Kayla.

"Alright," said Vicky. They changed into their clothes and went back to their lockers.

Amber came over to them. "I think Cindy deliberately bumped into me in class today. She also makes faces at me a lot. Maybe she stole my tiara," said Amber.

"She's one of our suspects, but we've got to hurry and get

fingerprints. We'll take yours first," said Vicky.

Amber pressed her fingers of her right hand on a black ink pad. Then she pressed her fingerprints on a fingerprint file card with her name on it. Then Amber did the same thing with her left hand and wiped the ink off her fingers with a wipe.

"See ya," said Amber, walking away.

Kayla walked over to Megan. "Hi, could you hold my comic book for a second while I take a sip from my water bottle?" she asked.

"Oh, okay," said Megan, holding the book.

"Thanks," said Kayla as Megan handed it back to her. Kayla went to Cindy's locker. "Hi. Could you please hold my cup for a minute while I fix my barrette?" Kayla asked.

"Okay," said Cindy, holding the plastic cup with water in it.

"Thanks," said Kayla, taking back her cup.

"Hi," said Kayla, going over to Shanté. "Please hold my notebook for a minute. I want to take a drink from my water bottle."

Shanté shrugged. "Alright."

Kayla took a sip from it. Then Shanté gave the notebook back to her.

Kayla rushed back to her locker and stuck a label on each of the items the girls touched. Then she wrote their names on them. *That wasn't too hard*, thought Kayla.

Vicky came back with a water bottle that Amy touched and a hairbrush that Nicole held and labeled them.

"Too bad we couldn't get Julien or Dylan's fingerprints," whispered Kayla. They tossed all the items in a large ziplock bag.

"All the girls left now. Let's search for fingerprints on Amber's locker," said Vicky.

Shining the flashlight all over Amber's locker and on the bench, they looked for fingerprints. Kayla, wearing gloves, put special white powder on the fingerprints they found. The powder stuck on the fingerprints. She dusted away the excess powder with a brush. Then she put the lifting tape on each of them.

Vicki put on plastic gloves and started lifting up each tape with a fingerprint on it. Then she put them on a fingerprint specimen card labeled Amber's locker.

They dashed back to their lockers.

"Wow, they're real prints but only some are clear," said Vicky.

"Now we'll remove the fingerprints from all of our items the girls touched," said Kayla.

They sat on a bench. They put the white powder and lifting tape on the fingerprints they found on each of the girl's items. Then they removed each tape and put the fingerprints of each girl on separate cards. They wrote down the name of the girl on the card with her fingerprints on it.

"Wow, we've got good fingerprints," said Vicky. "This wasn't easy."

"Shh, I hear someone coming," Kayla said, her heart racing. They hid under a bench.

They waited for a few minutes.

"Phew! I don't think anyone is coming. We better hurry and finish this," Vicky said.

"The kit has one magnifying glass, and I brought an extra one that I already had," Kayla said, handing Vicky one of them.

"What do we do next?" Vicky asked.

"Now we have to compare the fingerprints on Amber's locker and on the bench to each girl's fingerprints on her fingerprint specimens card," said Kayla.

"There are no matches," Vicky said, examining all the fingerprints through the magnifying glass.

"I don't see any matches either," Kayla said.

Vicky looked at all the fingerprints again. "Oh, Amber's fingerprints on her card matches the ones on her own locker," she said.

They looked at each other and started giggling.

Kayla carefully examined the fingerprints again through her magnifying glass. "Hey, look, Cindy's fingerprint on the plastic cup matches one of the fingerprints on Amber's locker," she gasped.

Vicky's hazel eyes with gold and green flecks opened wide. "Yes, it's a match!" she exclaimed, looking through the magnifying glass.

"Cindy could have stolen the tiara. She's jealous of Amber, and she seems to idolize Amy," said Kayla.

"This only proves that Cindy touched Amber's locker, but it's still a good clue," said Vicky.

They cleaned up and quickly tossed everything into

Kayla's large, blue backpack.

Then they dashed out of the ballet school.

"I'll see you next week in ballet, and we'll look for more clues. Bye," Vicky said.

"Bye," said Kayla, walking toward her house.

Chapter Four

CLASHING SWORDS AT THE AUDITIONS

Zooming home after school the following week, Kayla ran downstairs into the den. "Grandma, tomorrow are the auditions," she said.

Grandma looked up from the book she was reading. "You've been practicing every night. Just do your best," she said.

The following afternoon, Mr. Glasser stood on the stage in the auditorium in school.

"Everybody please be quiet. We'll now have the auditions. Mrs. Melon, my assistant, and I will announce what role we're auditioning for. Whoever wants to try out for our hero, George, who rescues the princess, come to the front now," said Mr. Glasser.

Several boys tried out for George.

"Next are the tryouts for Princess Emma," said Mr. Glasser.

Kayla and nine other girls sat in the first row.

Some of the girls read Princess Emma's part very softly. *I can hardly hear them*, thought Kayla.

Many students clapped when Shannon finished reading her lines.

Shannon acted pretty well. I'm sure she'll get the part, thought Kayla.

Kayla was last to try out for the princess. She started reading very softly, her heart pounding. After awhile, she forgot about the audience and felt like she was Princess Emma.

Kayla went back to her seat. "You'd make a great princess, but the competition is fierce," smiled Marissa.

"I was the best. I know I'll get the princess role," said Shannon to Julie and Grace.

"Next is Captain Red Fox," Mrs. Melon called out, motioning the boys with her hand to sit in the front.

Several boys tried out for the captain.

When it was Matthew's turn, he really sounded like the evil captain.

Everyone clapped their hands.

"Whoever is trying out for the princess' ladies-in-waiting, Ella, Ida and Anna, come up now," said Mr. Glasser.

Then it was Marissa's turn to try out for Meg, Princess Emma's younger sister. She was poised and at ease while she read her lines.

"All the girls who are trying out for Queen Anne, sit in the first row now," called out Mrs. Melon.

Several girls tried out for the queen.

"Next are the tryouts for Hammer Head, Snuff and Hawk Eye, the captain's three top meanest pirates," said Mr. Glasser.

First each boy had to read the script. Then they all fought with plastic swords.

"Whoever wants to try out for Count Ralph, come up now," called out Mr. Glasser.

When the boys finished reading Count Ralph's part, many girls tried out for Princess Emma's governess, Hilda.

"I think Crystal was best," Marissa said.

Kayla nodded. "I hope she gets the part."

Then many boys tried out for the three sword makers, who were George's friends.

Mr. Glasser stood on the stage. "The auditions are finished now. Mrs. Melon and I will decide what roles you'll get. Only some of the students will get the lead roles. The rest will get the smaller roles. We will also have stagehands, who will be in charge of painting, making props and changing scenery. Tomorrow afternoon I'll hang up a poster outside the auditorium with the casting list," said Mr. Glasser.

The next day when school was over, Kayla headed for the auditorium.

A lot of students were already crowding around the poster. When she got close, Kayla saw her name next to Princess Emma.

I can't believe I'm the princess, thought Kayla.

Marissa came over and saw her name next to Meg.

"We got the parts we wanted," said Marissa.

"I'm so excited," smiled Kayla.

Crystal looked at the poster. "I'm Hilda, the governess," she said to Kayla and Marissa.

"Hey, I'm Captain Red Fox," laughed Matthew.

"I got the part of one of the captain's top pirates Snuff," shouted Jamal.

"Hey, I got the lead role as handsome George," Andrew said.

"And I'm that rich dude, Count Ralph," said Eddie.

Shannon came over and started to read the poster.

"What! There must be a mistake. I should be the princess, not Kayla. Oh no, I only got the role of the queen," she said angrily to Grace and Julie.

Julie frowned. "Grace and I are only ladies-in-waiting. But we like our parts."

Shannon's hazel eyes narrowed. "I don't want a small part. I'm a great actress," she said, dashing away.

"Shannon is such a snob. Queen Anne is a good role. But you know Shannon. She has to be the star," said Marissa with a frown.

Marissa and Kayla stepped on the leaves in the bright sun as they walked home together.

Kayla ran downstairs to the big den when she got home. Her grandma was watching TV.

"I'm going to be Princess Emma," said Kayla.

"I knew you could do it," said her grandma.

"I never got such a big part. I hope I don't mess it up," said Kayla. "Will you practice with me?" she asked.

"Of course!" said Grandma.

Oliver started barking. Kayla picked him up and twirled around the room.

Chapter Five

COSTUME DANCE

Friday night, Kayla walked into the living room.

"You look like a real princess," said her grandma.

Kayla wore a yellow, silk dress, low open-toed gold heels, gold hoop pierced earrings and a gold metal crown on her head. She was dressed for the Halloween dance.

"I hear a car honking," Grandma said.

"It's Sarah's mom," said Kayla, peeking out the window.

"Bye Grandma," said Kayla, hugging her.

Kayla climbed into the car, and Mrs. Levy drove to Island Hills Middle School.

"Have a good time," said Mrs. Levy when she dropped off the girls in the parking lot.

When they walked into the gym, there were paper skeletons, bats, ghosts and orange and black streamers hanging from the high ceiling. Orange and black balloons, in gold weights, were on the refreshment tables.

Sarah's green eyes lit up. "Look at the white spiderwebs hanging all over the windows and walls. The gym looks so spooky and haunted." She wore a long green dress, low black heels and a gold crown on her wavy red hair.

They joined Breanna and Marissa, who were standing by

tables filled with refreshments. There were cakes, cookies, candies, soda, small water bottles and a huge bowl of fruit punch.

"Hi," said Breanna, wearing a short purple dress, black high heels and a gold crown on her head.

"We're all dressed like princesses," laughed Marissa, wearing a short white dress, low silver heels and a gold crown.

"Our crowns remind me of Amber's tiara. Vicky and I found a new clue. Cindy's fingerprint was on Amber's locker," Kayla told her friends.

"Why would she steal the tiara?" asked Sarah.

"Because she seems to worship Amy and wants her to have the star role," said Kayla.

"Cindy's fingerprint is not enough evidence," said Breanna.

Kayla nodded, "I agree with you."

Just then Andrew came over to the table and drank a cup of fruit punch.

The DJ put on a CD with slow music on the stereo system.

Andrew turned to Marissa. "Would you like to dance with me?"

"Sure," smiled Marissa.

Then Tyrone walked over to Breanna. "Hi, do you wanna dance?"

"Okay," Breanna said.

"Omigosh! Breanna's crown fell off. Tyrone just picked it

up," laughed Sarah.

"Hey, a lot of boys and girls are doing a group dance now. Everyone does the same steps at the same time. C'mon, let's join them," suggested Kayla.

"No thanks. I'm not a good dancer," Sarah answered.

Kayla joined one of the long lines and followed the others. They swayed to the right and then to the left. They spun around, clapping their hands and waving their arms to the music.

When the dance ended, Kayla saw Jason standing near the refreshment table. *I'll say hello to him*, she thought, walking over there. She tried to avoid walking in a puddle of red fruit punch on the floor but a boy bumped into her. She slipped on the sticky punch and fell to the ground. One of her gold heels fell off. Her dress was splattered with red punch.

"Are you okay?" Marissa asked.

Kayla looked up and saw Jason staring at her. Then other girls and boys started looking at her. Some were laughing. She grabbed her shoe and ran to the girls' bathroom. Marissa ran after her.

"I'm so embarrassed," said Kayla, tears rolling down her cheeks.

"Whoever saw you fall will forget about it in a little while," said Marissa.

"I'll try to get some of the punch off my dress," said Kayla, pouring water on it from the sink.

"C'mon, let's get some snacks," said Marissa.

Standing at the refreshment table, Kayla saw Jason and Shannon dancing a slow dance. "Oh, no, snobby Shannon also has a crush on Jason. Her blow dried, shoulder-length blond hair and her red cheerleading outfit looks so perfect," whispered Kayla to Marissa.

Mrs. Chandler, one of the teachers, waved her arms and the music stopped. "It's time to choose the two best costumes at our costume dance," she said, talking into the microphone. "Second place goes to Cassie, who is dressed like an alien from outer space. First place goes to Jamie Lee, our three-headed dragon," she said.

Everyone cheered and clapped. Some of the boys whistled.

"Here are your rewards," said Mrs. Chandler. Cassie and Jamie Lee each got a gift certificate to a department store.

Kayla stood alone against the wall.

Jason walked over to her. "Hi Kayla. You must be a princess with that crown on your head."

Kayla nodded her head. "I like your black Ninja costume."

Jason's big brown eyes lit up. "Thanks," he said. "I take karate lessons, and I hope to get a black belt someday."

"Wow," you must be really strong," said Kayla.

"Wanna dance?" he asked.

"Okay," smiled Kayla.

They started dancing to slow music.

I can't believe this. I'm really dancing with Jason. His

hands are warm and sweaty, but I don't care, thought Kayla.

She looked up and saw Shannon standing in a corner, glaring at her.

Shannon looks mad jealous, thought Kayla.

When the song was over, Jason grinned. "That was fun. I'll see you later," and he walked away.

Sarah went over to Kayla. "Let's go. My mother is picking us up at 11:00," she said.

"How was the dance?" asked Mrs. Levy as she was driving to Kayla's house.

"Good," Kayla answered.

"It was alright, but I like playing basketball better," Sarah said.

They all laughed together.

"Thank you Mrs. Levy. I'll see you in school, Sarah," Kayla said when they reached her house.

"Bye," Mrs. Levy and Sarah called out.

Chapter Six

A FIRST TOUGH GAME

Vicky and Kayla went to their dressing room after ballet class on Wednesday afternoon. They went into the dressing booths to change back into their clothes.

They sat on a long wooden bench across from their lockers. Kayla started reading her small detective notebook. "Cindy's fingerprint on Amber's locker," Kayla read out loud.

"Hi," said Amber, sitting on the bench next to them. "My parents and I made this poster," she said, holding it up.

The poster said:

Missing gold, jeweled Tiara.

Monetary reward for any information leading to its recovery.

Please email me at Amber.Armstrong@gmail.com

"What are you going to do with it?" asked Kayla.

"I'm going to ask Madame to hang it up in the waiting room. Many parents pick up their children there, and everyone will get to see it," said Amber.

"That's a very good idea," said Vicky.

"I was wondering what the person did with my tiara after they took it from my ballet bag," Amber said.

"They must have gone to their locker and stashed the tiara in their backpack," said Kayla.

"A boy could also have sneaked into the girls' dressing room and stolen the tiara. Then he could have put it in his locker," Amber said.

"Whoever stole it made believe they were taking a break to go to the bathroom or getting a drink from the water fountain or their water bottle," Vicky said.

"Do you want us to come with you to show Madame the poster?" asked Kayla.

"Yes, please come," said Amber.

They walked down the aisle toward the front exit of the dressing room. Cindy and Amy were talking at their lockers.

"Let's stand here and listen to Cindy and Amy talking," whispered Vicky to Amber and Kayla.

"I practice my ballet steps almost every night for the Sugar Plum Fairy and Marie," said Amy.

"You are a wonderful ballerina. You should have gotten the part as Marie," said Cindy.

"Cindy really admires Amy. She's always complimenting her about her dancing," said Amber in a low voice.

"I wonder if Cindy stole your tiara and would even hurt you so Amy could get the part as Marie," whispered Vicky.

"I guess it's possible," whispered Amber.

The girls went into Madame's office in the waiting room.

"Could you hang up this poster?" asked Amber.

Madame read the poster. "I'd be glad to. I'll do anything

to help you get back your tiara," she said.

"Thank you," said Amber.

"Amber, I chose you to be Marie because you're the best dancer for the part. You don't need your tiara to dance well," Madame said.

"I guess so, but I felt that the tiara gave me good luck," Amber said.

Then Madame put special tape on the back of the poster and hung it up on a wall in the waiting room.

"Let us know if anyone calls you about the tiara," said Kayla.

"Okay. I've got to go now. My mom's driving me home. Bye," said Amber, leaving the school.

"Someone may give us information to get the reward," said Vicky as she and Kayla walked out the front door.

Kayla nodded. "It could lead us to the thief. I'll see you at our next class," said Kayla.

"Bye," said Vicky.

That night at 6:00, Kayla and Marissa walked into the Island Hills Middle School gym.

"Wow, what a huge crowd," Kayla said.

They sat on the bleachers, close to the basketball court.

Marissa put on her light blue-framed eye glasses. "I'm nearsighted so I have to wear glasses for distance."

The seventh-grade girls' home team, the Island Hills Leopards, wearing white uniforms trimmed with navy blue, and the Panthers, wearing red uniforms trimmed with white, from Oakland Middle School, ran onto the court. Both teams started shooting baskets to warm-up.

Matthew, Jamal, Tyrone, and Crystal raced up the narrow steps and sat next to Kayla and Marissa.

The referee blew his whistle and threw up the ball. Destiny, the Leopard center, tipped the ball to Sarah. Sarah passed to Lakeysha.

"Pass it to me," yelled Breanna. Lakeysha shot the ball 20 feet away. It hit the rim and bounced off.

"Why didn't Lakeysha pass the ball to me? I was much closer to the basket," said Breanna to Sarah.

"You're right," said Sarah.

The Panthers had a hot streak and led by eight points at the end of the first quarter.

Destiny took the ball, dribbling upcourt and passed to Sarah. A Panther guard got behind Sarah and stole the ball, dribbling fast downcourt. She threw the ball 20 feet away from the basket. It went in.

"Why can't you hold onto the ball, Butterfingers," yelled Lakeysha.

Sarah gave her a dirty look and tears rolled down her cheeks.

The Panthers led by ten points at halftime.

Matthew shook his head. "The Leopards are not playing well."

"Duh, no kidding," said Jamal.

When the whistle blew, the third quarter began.

Destiny took the ball and bounced it to Breanna. Breanna, with number 10 on her jersey, tossed the ball, and it went through the net.

"Hooray, Leopards," yelled the fans.

When Erin was dribbling the ball upcourt, a Panther stole the ball and shot 20 feet away. It went in.

"You jerk, why can't you hold onto the ball," Lakeysha yelled at Erin. Then she pushed her.

Then Erin punched Lakeysha on her arm.

The referee, wearing a black and white striped shirt and black pants, blew his whistle. "You're both out of the game," he yelled.

The Leopard fans booed.

Lakeysha and Erin sat on the bench.

"There will be no fighting on my team," Coach Taylor said to them. Then the coach put in Salena and Jennifer.

"The Leopards should pass more to each other," said Crystal.

"And make more baskets," said Marissa.

At the end of the third quarter, the Leopards trailed by ten points.

During the fourth quarter, the Leopards couldn't stop the Panthers from making baskets.

With one minute to go, Jennifer dribbled the ball upcourt and passed to Sarah. Sarah passed to Destiny who passed to Salena. Salena threw the ball up high toward their basket. But it went flying into the bleachers.

"You have to aim for the basket," Destiny yelled at Salena.

"Sorry," Salena said.

The horn blew loudly. The game was over.

Tyrone looked up at the electric scoreboard. "The final score is Panthers 54 to Leopards 40."

Both coaches shook hands.

The Leopards shook hands with the Panthers and headed to their locker room to shower and change into their clothes.

Kayla and Marissa said good-bye to their friends and went to the parking lot in back of the school. They hopped into Mrs. Diaz's silver car.

"Hello, how was the game?" asked Marissa's mother.

"The Leopards lost the game," said Marissa. "But Breanna and Sarah were good."

Marissa turned on the radio, and they listened to music on the way to Kayla's house.

When they reached her house, Marissa said, "Adiós amiga, which means in Spanish, good-bye friend. You know my family speaks English and Spanish because we're from Peru."

"Adiós amigas," Kayla said.

"Adiós," Mrs. Diaz and Marissa said together, smiling.

Chapter Seven

PIRATE'S TRICK

On Halloween night, Kayla, Sarah, Breanna, Andrew, Jamal and Matthew were standing on the front porch of Marissa's house. The cold October wind blew orange, red and yellow leaves all over the grass. A huge Jack O'Lantern was glowing on the window sill.

Marissa and her seven year old brother, José, came out of the house. José was dressed as Spider Man.

"I'm going trick or treating with you," said José, holding up an extra large green treat bag. "I want to get lots and lots of candy."

"My mother told me that José has to come along with us," frowned Marissa.

The girls were all dressed as witches, wearing long black dresses, green stockings, black boots and pointed black hats. Andrew and Matthew wore vampire masks with fake blood coming out of their mouths and long red capes. Jamal wore a skeleton costume and a mask.

"Hee-hee-hee, let's fly to old Mrs. Hester's house, and we'll get her homemade candied apples," cackled Breanna, holding her broom.

"You're lucky. You have a magic broom," said José.

When they reached Mrs. Hester's old house, Matthew knocked on her door. A gray-haired, short woman opened the door. She grinned at them, showing her yellowish teeth.

"Hee-hee-hee-heee! I'm glad you kids came for another Halloween," she cackled. She gave each one of them a red candied apple on a stick, covered with wax paper.

They passed kids on the streets dressed as goblins, mummies, monsters and Batman. They went trick-or-treating, loading their treat bags with candies, nuts, dried and fresh fruit and real coins.

Then three girls dressed as princesses, with crowns on their heads, walked towards them. *Those princesses' crowns remind me of Amber's tiara. I really want to find her tiara. Vicky and I must search for new clues,"* thought Kayla.

"Boo, boo, boo," yelled two boys, dressed as ghosts, jumping out of the bushes.

Marissa screamed. They all laughed.

They walked down the street until they got to a big house on the corner.

"Let's not go in that house. I heard it was haunted," Sarah said.

"It sure looks haunted. It needs to be painted, shingles are missing, and the stairs to the porch are broken," said Matthew.

"Oh look, there's a broken window on the second floor. I wonder if anyone lives there?" Andrew wanted to know.

"I'm going to knock on the door," said Matthew. "Who wants to come with me?"

They all shook their heads no.

"Chickens, I dare you to go in," said Matthew.

"I I I'll go," stammered Jamal.

Matthew and Jamal walked up the broken stairs. Matthew knocked on the door, but no one answered. José ran after them.

"Come back here," yelled Marissa.

Matthew opened the door, and the three boys went in.

"I wonder what's going on in there. Oh, no, I saw something purple in the window," cried Marissa.

They waited for several minutes.

Then Matthew, Jamal and José flew out of the house and ran down the street. The others followed them.

"What happened in there?" asked Marissa.

"It was very dark, but something touched my arm. I think it was a ghost," José frowned.

"I felt something slimy touch my hand," said Jamal. "Maybe it was a goblin. Yuck."

"We heard squeaking noises and a door slammed shut. Then we ran out." said Matthew.

"Eww, you're all full of spiderwebs," said Marissa.

"And dusty cobwebs," added Breanna.

Matthew, Jamal and José started brushing them off their clothes.

"Eww, a spiderweb blew on me," said Kayla.

"I really think that house is haunted," said Jamal.

"Uh-huh," José agreed.

"Hey, we're in front of Mrs. Munster's house," Andrew told them.

"Let's skip her house. She never gives out any treats to the kids. I've even heard Mrs. Munster may be a real witch," said Jamal with a laugh.

"Look at those three big boys in pirate costumes. They're spraying red and orange paint on the side of her house," said Kayla.

"Let's get out of here before she blames us," cried Sarah.

They raced down the street. The three pirates ran after them. Suddenly, one of the pirates, wearing a red scarf wrapped around his head and a black patch on one eye, grabbed José's treat bag. Then the three pirates ran away.

"Gimme back my candy," shouted José, running after them.

"José, come back here," yelled Marissa.

But José didn't listen and ran after the pirates. They followed José. The pirates and José ran into the cemetery. When they finally caught up with José, the pirates were gone.

"José, I told you not to run after those bad boys," said Marissa.

"I'm sorry," said Jose.

"It's pitch dark outside except for the moon and the stars," said Andrew.

"Eek, look at all the tombstones," shrieked Sarah.

Just then, they heard groaning noises and loud footsteps. As the footsteps got louder, strange voices said, "boo, boo, booooo."

They didn't move.

"I see white things flying in the air," gasped Kayla.

"They're ghosts," gasped Marissa.

They all screamed.

"Let's get out of here," yelled Matthew.

"Hurry up," shouted Andrew.

José grabbed Marissa's broom. Then they all started running past the tombstones and out of the cemetery. They were all panting out of breath by the time they got to Marissa's house.

They told Mrs. Diaz all about their adventures.

"Wow, what an exciting time you had," said Mrs. Diaz.

Marissa's small white dog with golden-brown patches on her ears and body jumped up on Andrew.

"What's her name?" asked Andrew, stroking her back.

"Missy," said Marissa.

"Mommy, the pirates took all my candy," said José.

"I'm sure Marissa will share her candy with you," said Mrs. Diaz.

Marissa nodded. "Oh, alright."

They listened to music from the stereo and danced in the huge living room. They ate donuts with chocolate and orange icing, ice cream cones, candy and drank apple juice and soda.

"Come on everyone. It's late. I'll drive all of you home now. Marissa, stay here with José," said Mrs. Diaz.

"Alright, but there better not be any ghosts coming in our house. I wish dad were still living with us," whispered Marissa to her mom.

"At least you and José visit him every other weekend now that we're divorced," said Mrs. Diaz softly to Marissa.

Marissa's friends grabbed their treat bags. "Goodbye," they said to Marissa and José.

They all scrambled into the car. "Thank you," they all said together.

"You're welcome. I'm glad you all had fun tonight," said Mrs. Diaz.

They passed houses lit up with pumpkins, skeletons, monsters, ghosts, witches, bats and all sorts of Halloween decorations as Mrs. Diaz drove them to their houses.

Chapter Eight

LOOKING THROUGH THE MAGNIFYING GLASS

K ayla and the other students were doing their exercises at the barre in the ballet studio.

"Come to the centre of the room now," said Madame Sofia.

She turned on slow music. They did several exercises in the centre of the studio.

"Now do pirouettes," Madame said.

The music got faster. The dancers twirled around the room.

Amber fell on the floor.

"Ow, someone bumped into me," moaned Amber.

"You just got dizzy," laughed Nicole.

"Are you alright," asked Madame.

"My knee hurts a little, but it's okay," said Amber.

"Phew. Thank goodness!" exclaimed Madame. "Now let's practice our leaps."

"Can we skip the leaps and just start rehearsing for the Nutcracker?" asked Julien.

"Julien, stop complaining," said Madame with a frown. "It's hard work to become a good ballet dancer. I went to a full-time ballet school and danced in the corps de ballet."

"You're right, Madame," Julien agreed.

"Now line up for your leaps," said Madame. They did small leaps and then large leaps across the shiny floor.

When they finished their leaps, everyone stood in front of Madame.

"When is our performance?" asked Tamara.

"It's already November. Our performance will be at the end of December. Let's start rehearsing. Now everyone sit against the mirrored walls and wait until it's your turn to perform," Madame said.

When the dancers finished practicing Act 2, they stood in front of Madame Sofia.

"We'll start rehearsing at our dance theater next door about two weeks before the dress rehearsal with the entire cast with the other classes in the Nutcracker Ballet. By the way, a director from a full-time dance school will attend our performance of the Nutcracker Ballet. He may select some of my students to audition at his school. I'll see you next week," Madame smiled.

The girls curtsied and the boys bowed to Madame and went to their dressing rooms.

After Vicky and Kayla changed their clothes, they sat on a bench near their lockers.

"Let's check our suspect list," said Vicky.

Kayla took out her detective notebook. "Amy and Megan are our two main suspects. Our other suspects are Julien, Dylan and Cindy."

"Anyone else?" asked Vicky.

Just then, the janitor, with a black mustache, started sweeping the floor near their lockers.

They stared at him. "Maybe the janitor took the tiara," said Kayla, adding him to the list.

"Let's interview the suspects now," said Vicky.

They found Megan combing her curly, long, dark brown hair by her locker.

"Megan, would you have any idea who stole Amber's tiara?" asked Kayla.

"No, but it's such a beautiful tiara," said Megan.

"Wouldn't you like to be Marie?" asked Kayla.

"Of course! Wouldn't anyone? I'm the best dancer in the class, and I'm sure I'll get into a full time ballet school," bragged Megan.

"If Amber couldn't dance, then you or Amy would get to be Marie," said Vicky.

"Are you accusing me of taking her tiara?" asked Megan.

Vicky shook her head. "No, of course not."

"I've got to leave now," said Megan. She picked up her ballet bag and dashed off.

Amy was combing her curly, light brown hair when Kayla and Vicky walked over to her.

"Is this barrette yours?" asked Vicky, holding up the gold barrette they found.

"No," said Amy.

"Did you see anyone near Amber's locker on the day her

tiara was stolen?" asked Kayla.

"No, but we all took breaks during class that day. Amber was stupid to leave it in her ballet bag on the bench," said Amy.

"Do you wish you could be Marie?" asked Kayla.

"Yes, I'd love to be the star of the ballet. And my mom would really be proud of me. Why are you acting like detectives?" asked Amy.

"Amber asked us to help her get her tiara back," said Vicky.

They walked to the boys' dressing room and waited outside.

"Julien," yelled out Kayla.

Julien walked out. "Were you calling me?"

"Umm, yeah. Can we talk to you for a minute?" asked Kayla.

"Okay, shoot," said Julien.

"Do you know who would steal Amber's tiara or want to stop her from dancing Marie?" asked Vicky.

"Umm, no not really. Who cares about a dumb tiara anyway?" said Julien.

"The tiara is important to Amber. Wouldn't you want your sister to be Marie?" asked Kayla.

"Yeah, I wish Amy was Marie. My mom is really disappointed that Amy didn't get the star role. Anyway, who do you think you are, secret agents?" Julien asked.

"No, we're just trying to help Amber," explained Vicky.

"If I find out anything, I'll let you know," he said.

"Thanks. Could you tell Dylan we want to talk to him?" asked Vicky.

"Oh, okay," Julien said, going into the dressing room.

Dylan came out a few minutes later. "Hi girls. What's up?"

"Do you have any idea who took Amber's tiara," asked Vicky.

"I don't have a clue," Dylan said.

"Do you think Amy did it so she could become Marie?" asked Kayla.

Dylan looked puzzled. "Amy's too nice. Megan's also an understudy for Marie, so maybe she did it. Whoever did it must be mad jealous. Good luck with your detective work," laughed Dylan, and he walked away.

They rushed back to the girls' dressing room and went over to Cindy's locker.

"Do you have any idea who would take Amber's tiara or hurt her?" asked Kayla.

"No, but whoever did it is very mean," said Cindy, putting her stringy, brown hair into a pony tail with a white hair band.

"Wouldn't you rather have Amy or Megan be Marie?" asked Vicky.

Cindy's small brown eyes widened. "I think Amy is the best dancer. Amy should be Marie, but Madame chose Amber," she said, and she stalked out of the room.

Just then Nicole passed them. "Nicole," called Vicky. "Do

you know anything about who stole Amber's tiara?"

Nicole's hazel eyes narrowed. "No, I don't."

"Have you noticed anyone acting suspicious?" asked Kayla.

"Umm, no, but Amy really wanted to be Marie. I heard Amy tell Cindy that Amy is sure Madame would choose her to be Marie if Amber loses the part. I've got to go," said Nicole, walking away.

Kayla and Vicky sat on the bench in front of their lockers.

"I think Megan may have done it. She just has a small part in the Dance of Hot Chocolate," said Kayla, eating a granola bar.

"Amy and Megan are the understudies for Marie. Either one of them could have done it," said Vicky, sipping her bottle of apple juice.

"The role of Marie must be very important for Madame to have two understudies," said Kayla.

Vicky sighed. "I guess Madame's right. If one understudy got sick, what would she do?"

Kayla nodded her head. "Two understudies are better for the star role."

"Maybe it's someone we'd be least likely to suspect, like Nicole. I think she's jealous of Amber," Vicky said.

"It could also be Shanté because she's friends with Megan and Amy," said Kayla.

"Shanté's too nice to hurt anyone," sighed Vicky.

"When you're a detective, you can't assume anything.

I'm still adding Shanté and Nicole to the suspect list," said Kayla.

"It's very quiet now. I think everybody's gone. Let's look for more clues," said Vicky.

"One of the light bulbs keeps flickering on and off. Oh no, it went out. Now there's only one light bulb on. It's too dark in here. I'll get my flashlight and my magnifying glass from my detective kit," said Kayla.

Vicky shined the flashlight under Amber's locker. "I don't see anything," Vicky said. Then she started shining the flashlight under all the other lockers in the same row as Amber's.

"Go back. I think I saw something under the locker next to Amber's," said Kayla. Vicky shined the flashlight while Kayla squatted down and stretched her arm all the way under the locker.

"I've got it," Kayla said, holding up a small jewel.

"It sparkles just like a real diamond from Amber's tiara," said Vicky, looking through the magnifying glass.

Kayla held up the diamond and peered through the magnifying glass. "It looks like the same size and shape from the tiara. And it's under Cindy's locker," she said.

"The diamond could have been pushed around all over the place," said Vicky.

"It's a new clue. I'll save it," said Kayla, putting it into her jean pocket.

"I hear something banging over there," said Vicky.

They walked toward the loud noise and looked into the

big metal garbage pail. Just then, something dashed out of it.

"Eeek, a mouse," cried Kayla. They started screaming.

"Anybody here?" yelled the janitor. "I thought I heard someone screaming," he mumbled, holding his broom.

"Let's hide," said Vicky. They quickly hid under a long wood bench.

They heard the janitor walking around the room. They saw his black shoes, passing by their bench. Vicky started to cough and put her hand over her mouth.

I wish he'd leave already, thought Kayla, her heart pounding.

"Eww, a mouse," mumbled the janitor, trying to hit it with his broom. But the mouse scurried out of the room. The janitor ran after it.

Vicky and Kayla dashed quickly out the front door, and the door slammed behind them.

"Phew, I'm glad we didn't get caught," said Kayla, breathing deeply. "Nicole gave us new evidence that Amy believes that if Amber can't dance, she'll be Marie."

"I think Amy's our number one suspect right now," said Vicky.

"See ya. Bye," said Kayla, and she started running to her house.

That night, Kayla started tossing and turning in her bed, drifting off to sleep.

All at once, Kayla was the Sugar Plum Fairy dancing on her toes with the prince. The prince lifted her up in the air and gently placed her down. Then she started spinning around and crashed into the prince. They both fell on the floor. The prince looked at her in horror and vanished. Then she looked up and saw everyone in the audience laughing at her. Tears rolled down her cheeks as she leaped off the stage.

Kayla sat up in her bed. Her face was wet from sweating. She looked at her alarm clock.

It's 3:00 in the morning. I must have had a nightmare, she thought.

Then she tossed and turned in her bed and fell back to sleep.

Chapter Nine

GHOST'S SLEEPOVER

On Saturday evening, Kayla's mom drove Breanna, Sarah and Kayla to Marissa's house.

"Enjoy your sleepover," Mrs. Murphy said.

"Thank you Mrs. Murphy," said the girls to Kayla's mom, climbing out of the car.

"Hello," Mrs. Diaz said as they walked into the house.

Marissa led the girls downstairs into the den.

Her dog Missy jumped up on Sarah's lap.

"What kind of dog is she?" asked Sarah, patting her head.

"She's a Cavalier King Charles Spaniel," said Marissa.

"That's a big name for a small dog," laughed Sarah.

"What should we do first? I rented some really scary horror movies," said Marissa.

"We can watch movies later on. Why don't we put nail polish on our fingernails and toenails now," suggested Kayla.

"And do our hair," added Marissa.

They headed upstairs in the large split level house to Marissa's bedroom. The girls put their overnight bags and sleeping bags in the big closet with sliding doors.

Sarah painted her fingernails and toenails a deep purple.

Breanna frowned. "My nails are broken." She took out a

fake set of fingernails from her bag. She glued them on her finger nails. Then she painted her finger and toenails hot pink.

Marissa and Kayla put red nail polish on their finger and toenails.

"My mom works as a hair stylist at a hair salon. She taught me how to do some cool styles. Who's first?" asked Marissa.

"Meee! Please, give me a French braid," said Breanna.

"Sure," Marissa said, putting Breanna's hair into a braid.

"Breanna, you've got one thick, shiny black braid," said Kayla, smiling.

"That's nice. Can you put my hair in a French braid, too?" asked Sarah.

Marissa also put Sarah's red hair in a French braid.

"I want to have my hair in curls," said Kayla.

Marissa heated up a lot of small curlers and put them in Kayla's and her hair for several minutes. When Marissa removed the curlers, Kayla had a bunch of blond curls, and Marissa had a lot of dark brown curls.

Then they put on powder, mascara, rouge and lipstick.

"Hey Sarah, the powder covered up your freckles," laughed Breanna.

"That's okay," Sarah said.

Then they watched two horror movies on the DVD player in the den.

"The vampire movie was the scariest. There was so much blood," said Sarah.

"Don't worry. It's only fake blood," said Breanna.

"Now, let's dance," said Marissa.

They danced all around the living room to disco, rap and hip hop music blasting from the stereo.

José sneaked in and started dancing.

"José, puleeze go back to bed," said Marissa.

"Can I have some snacks first?" asked José.

"Okay," Marissa said, rolling her wide brown eyes.

Then they all went into the dining room.

On the long oval table were sandwiches cut in halves, salsa dip with taco chips and potato pancakes with apple sauce.

"I brought some candy," said Breanna, taking out a brown paper bag. She poured all kinds of candies into a bowl and put it on the table.

Then the girls sat down at the table and started eating.

"Mmm, my egg salad sandwich is good," said Breanna.

"Please pass the lemonade," said Sarah.

At that moment, Missy jumped up, putting a ham and cheese sandwich into her mouth. Then she ran away.

"Watch the food. Missy will be back for me," warned Marissa.

They made their own ice cream sundaes with chocolate and strawberry syrup and whipped cream.

A cold gust of wind blew the paper napkins all over the room, and the curtains started flying all around.

"We'd better close the windows," said Sarah, putting a spoonful of butter pecan ice cream in her mouth.

"I think I just saw a figure that looked like a g g ghost at the window," stammered Marissa.

"I see a shadowy figure moving around," said Breanna. The girls started screaming. Breanna grabbed the bowl of candy, and they bounded upstairs to Marissa's bedroom.

"Let's calm down. I'm sure it wasn't a ghost. It could have been branches of a tree moving in the wind," Sarah said.

The girls changed into their nightgowns and sat on the soft, bright blue carpet. They started munching on the candy.

"Who wants to tell us a scary story?" Marissa wanted to know, biting into a gummy sour worm.

"I do. Umm, let me think. This is a story I heard in my sleepover camp in Massachusetts last summer," said Breanna. "There were a lot of boys and girls sitting around a campfire, singing songs and roasting marshmallows. A girl named Lonnie looked up and saw a girl smiling at her in the trees."

Breanna took a deep breath and chewed on some Skittles.

"So what happened next?" Marissa asked.

Breanna continued her story. "Then Lonnie got up and followed the girl to the lake. The girl said her name was Terry. Lonnie put her hand on the girl's shoulder. Lonnie's hand went through the girl's shoulder. 'You're a ghost', cried Lonnie to Terry."

"I'm getting the chills," said Sarah.

"Then Terry started to push Lonnie into the lake. But Lonnie ran back to her friends, and the girl ghost disappeared. That's the end of the story," said Breanna.

"That was a scary story," said Marissa.

"Someone c-c-close the closet doors. I think I saw something moving around in there," stammered Kayla.

"It could be a mouse or something," screamed Breanna. They ran downstairs and into the living room.

José came in wearing his batman pajamas. "What happened?" he asked.

"It's late. Go back to bed, José," Marissa commanded.

"But I heard you screaming, so I thought you saw a ghost," José said, and he ran upstairs to his bedroom.

Then the girls went upstairs to Marissa's bedroom.

"It's 3:00 in the morning," said Breanna, yawning. Marissa closed the sliding closet doors and turned off the lights. The girls snuggled into their sleeping bags and drifted off to sleep.

The next day, Mrs. Diaz came into the bedroom. "Wake up girls. It's 11:30 in the morning," she said.

After the girls got dressed, Marissa, Kayla and José helped Mrs. Diaz make breakfast. They mixed eggs, flour, milk and baking powder together and poured the batter into the frying pan. They made big, round pancakes and stacked them on plates. Mrs. Diaz made bacon. Sarah and Breanna set the dining room table.

When they finished eating their breakfast, the girls put the dishes in the dishwasher.

"Mom, can my friends stay longer?" asked Marissa.

"Alright," said Mrs. Diaz.

"Let's watch another movie now," said Kayla.

The girls ran downstairs to the den. Missy started barking and followed them.

They watched a science fiction movie about aliens from outer space. Then they played games. The stereo played CDs as they danced to jazz, hip hop, rap and country music.

"Here's the pizza pie I ordered from a pizzeria," said Mrs. Diaz, bringing it to the den.

"Did you find the tiara yet?" asked Breanna, taking a bite of pizza with pepperoni on it.

Kayla shrugged, "No, but we have some suspects and clues."

"Try to trick them into telling you what they know about it," said Sarah, taking a second slice of pizza.

"It's time for you girls to go home," called out Mrs. Diaz.

"Good-bye Marissa," the girls said, leaving the house. Breanna, Sarah and Kayla scrambled into Mrs. Diaz's car.

"We had a very good time," Breanna said.

"Thank you," the girls said together.

"I'm glad you all enjoyed yourselves," said Mrs. Diaz.

They played music on the radio as Mrs. Diaz drove them home.

Chapter Ten

SLIPPERY ICE AND A BALL OF FUR

"Dad," yelled Kayla when she got off the train at the East Highland station in upstate New York.

"This is the first time you've taken the train alone. How was your trip?" asked her father.

"Good," said Kayla.

"Please call your mother and tell her you're here now," said her father, handing her his cell phone. She called her mother and left a message on her voice mail. Her dad put her suitcase in the trunk, and they climbed into his creamy tan SUV.

"We're going straight to your Aunt Carolyn and Uncle Brian's house for Thanksgiving dinner," said her dad.

When they arrived, Kayla leaped out the door and rang the door bell.

"Hello, Amanda," said Kayla, hugging her cousin. They went into the living room. Kayla hugged her aunt and uncle.

A big black Labrador Retriever jumped up on Kayla. "Hello Max," she said, patting his head.

Kayla's father walked over to his father, sitting on the couch. "Hi Dad. I'm glad you're living with Brian since Mom died. How's your arthritis?" he asked.

"Sometimes my knees and ankles feel stiff, and I have to use a cane," he said.

"I've missed you," said Kayla, hugging her grandpa.

"You've gotten a lot taller and you're so pretty," Grandpa said, proudly.

"Grandpa Joe, will you play checkers with me?" asked Kayla.

"Sure," Grandpa said.

"I play the winner," said Amanda. Kayla laid out the red and black checkers on the board.

"I'm red," said Kayla, starting to play.

When they each had two kings left, her grandfather jumped one of her red kings, and cornered her other king.

"Grandpa, you always beat me," said Kayla.

"I'll take the black checkers," said Amanda as she and her grandfather started to play. When her grandfather jumped Amanda's last black king, the game was over.

"Grandpa beat both of us," Kayla told her father.

"He used to beat me most of the time," he chuckled.

"Dinner's ready," called her aunt. Everyone sat down at the dining room table. Uncle Brian carved the turkey with an electric knife.

"Carolyn, you make the best stuffing," said Kayla's father, putting a forkful in his mouth.

"Mmm, the mashed sweet potatoes with marshmallows are delicious," said Kayla.

Aunt Carolyn put the chocolate pudding pie with whipped cream that she made on the table.

"Uncle Dan, my mom said you're taking Kayla and me skiing in Vermont during our winter vacation from school," said Amanda.

"Yes, that's right," said Kayla's dad.

"Hooray," said Kayla and Amanda in unison.

"Oh, we're going ice skating at the indoor ice skating rink on Saturday," said Amanda.

"Goody" said Kayla.

Kayla and her dad hugged everyone and said good-bye. When her father drove them home, they took the elevator up to the eleventh floor and went into his apartment.

Her dad's brown eyes lit up. "We're going to the movies with Alyssa tomorrow."

"Okay," she mumbled. *I wish Mom and Dad could get back together,* thought Kayla. She headed for her own bedroom and drifted off to sleep.

The next day, Kayla's dad drove to Alyssa's apartment building and parked in front. Alyssa was waiting outside for them.

"Hello, Kayla. I've been looking forward to meeting you," said Alyssa, sitting next to Kayla's father in the front seat.

"Hello," frowned Kayla.

When they walked into the movie theater, Kayla's dad sat between Alyssa and Kayla.

"Pass the popcorn," whispered Kayla to her father. The three of them laughed a lot during the movie.

"What a funny movie," said Alyssa, when it was over.

"Ladies, would you like to have a bite to eat?" asked her father.

"Yes," they answered.

Kayla sat across from her father and Alyssa in a booth at a diner.

"So, how do you like school," asked Alyssa, taking a bite of her bacon, lettuce and tomato sandwich.

"It's okay," mumbled Kayla.

"Omigosh, I forgot to tell you. My drama class is putting on a new play. I got the star role as Princess Emma," blurted out Kayla.

"Good for you!" beamed her dad.

"That's awesome," smiled Alyssa, pushing her short, straight brown hair away from her face.

"Oh, Daddy, Vicky and I haven't found the tiara yet. We're trying to catch the thief. We even took fingerprints, but we have to get more leads," said Kayla.

"Wow, you're still playing detective now," said her dad.

"Maybe I can help. Tell me about it," said Alyssa. Kayla told them what Vicky and she did so far.

"You should search the dressing room again and ask the suspects more questions to get more information. You may even catch one of them telling a lie," suggested Alyssa.

"Okay," said Kayla.

Then they dropped off Alyssa at her house and started driving home. "Are you in love with Alyssa?" asked Kayla.

"No, but I like her very much," said her dad.

I feel sad that my dad isn't with my mom anymore. But Alyssa is nice, thought Kayla.

On Saturday afternoon, Aunt Carolyn drove Kayla and Amanda to the indoor ice skating rink.

"My parents just bought me these new ice skates," said Amanda.

Kayla rented ice skates. Sitting on a bench, Kayla and Amanda put on their white ice skates.

When Kayla started to skate, she kept slipping on the ice. All she could do was hold onto the metal railing that went along the entire rink.

Amanda skated around the rink with ease. "Watch me," called out Amanda to Kayla.

Amanda was spinning around and skating backwards on the ice as the music blasted from the loud speakers.

"Wow, you're super! How did you become such a good skater?" asked Kayla.

"I've been skating since I was seven, and now I'm 11 years old. I've also been taking lessons for two years," said Amanda.

"I've only gone ice skating a few times. It's fun skating in an indoor ice skating rink," remarked Kayla.

"I like indoor and outdoor rinks," said Amanda, holding Kayla's hand and skating around the rink. Then Kayla started skating very slowly by herself.

"Try to skate faster," said Amanda, going behind Kayla and pushing her. They started skating very fast.

"Yikes, we're going to crash into that boy," Kayla yelled.

But it was too late. They smacked into the boy, and they all fell on the ice.

"I'm sorry," said Kayla to the boy.

"It's okay," the boy said. He scrambled himself up, and he quickly skated away.

Suddenly Amanda started coughing and wheezing and her face turned pale. "I I'm having an asthma attack. Get my inhaler from my j j jacket pocket," stammered Amanda, lying down on the ice.

Kayla grabbed the inhaler from Amanda's pocket. "Here it is," she said, handing it to her.

Amanda puffed on the inhaler several times. She took a deep breath. "I feel much better now," she said.

"Phew, I'm glad you're alright. Let's get hot dogs," said Kayla.

"I occasionally get asthma attacks now. I only take medication for it when I need it," said Amanda, sipping her hot chocolate. "But, when I was a baby, I used to get a lot of attacks. I always carry my inhaler, just in case I need it."

After Kayla returned her ice skates, they went to the parking lot and hopped into Amanda's mother's car.

"Mom, I had an asthma attack when I was ice skating, but I used my inhaler," blurted out Amanda.

"Oh dear, are you alright now?" asked her mother.

"I'm fine, Mom. You promised to buy me a pet today," said Amanda.

"Oh, alright. But you can only get a small animal," said her mom.

"Kayla, do you want to come with us?" asked Amanda.

"Yes," said Kayla and called her dad on her aunt's cell phone to tell him she'd come back later.

Amanda's mother drove to the shopping center.

"Girls, I'll meet you in the pet store in about 45 minutes. I have a few things to buy," said Amanda's mom. She parked her forest green car in the parking lot near the pet store.

The girls went into the pet store and downstairs where most of the animals were.

"Why don't you get a parakeet?" said Kayla, poking her finger into a cage full of parakeets.

"No, I think I want a hamster," said Amanda, walking over to a cage with two hamsters in it.

"They're so cute and small," said Kayla.

"Let's look at the guinea pigs," Amanda said.

They looked into a cage with two baby guinea pigs in it. One was white with brown patches all over it and the other one was only tan.

"May I please hold the guinea pig that's white and brown?" Amanda asked a saleswoman.

The saleswoman handed it to Amanda.

"Thanks Ellie," said Amanda to the saleswoman, who

was wearing a nametag on her shirt. Amanda patted its head and handed it to Kayla.

"It looks like a little ball of fur," said Kayla, holding the guinea pig with both hands.

Suddenly the guinea pig jumped out of Kayla's hands and scooted away. "I can't find him," screamed Kayla.

"It's a female and she's seven weeks old," Ellie called out. They started looking for her.

They looked under the cages, on shelves and all over the room.

"I found her," said Ellie, picking up the guinea pig beneath the hamster cage. She put her back into her cage.

"Hi girls," said Amanda's mother, walking over to them.

"Mom, may I have the white and brown guinea pig now or else someone else will buy her?" asked Amanda.

"Oh alright," Amanda's mom said.

"Ellie, we want to buy the white and brown guinea pig today," called Amanda.

"What do we need to buy for it?" asked her mom.

"First pick out a cage," said Ellie.

"I like this one," said Amanda, choosing a large cage made out of green wire. Then she picked out a metal bowl, a water bottle, a book about guinea pigs, a nestbox, nail clippers and a flea comb for her short-haired guinea pig.

"What do they eat?" asked Kayla.

"They need to eat fresh fruits, vegetables, hay and pellets," explained Ellie.

"Thank you for helping us," said Amanda.

"Good luck! Bye," said Ellie.

"Wow, having a guinea pig is quite expensive," exclaimed Amanda's mother, paying for everything on her credit card.

"What are you gonna name her?" asked Kayla as they drove back to her father's apartment.

"I'm gonna call her Daisy," said Amanda, holding the guinea pig in her cage on her lap.

"Oh, that's cute," said Kayla.

When they reached Kayla's dad's building, she buzzed his apartment. They waited for him to come down.

"Look at my guinea pig," said Amanda.

"It's adorable," said Kayla's dad.

"We've got to go now," said Aunt Carolyn. They all hugged each other.

"I'll call you or send you emails," said Amanda. Then her mother drove away.

On Sunday morning, Kayla's father was driving her to the train station. "Vicky and I better start searching right away for more clues," said Kayla.

"Let me know if you need any help with your detective work. Call me when you get home," said her father.

Kayla kissed her dad on his cheek. She pulled the handle, wheeling her suitcase over a gap and onto the train.

When she got to the train station in Manhattan, her mother was waiting for her on the platform.

"Hi, Kayla," said her mom, hugging her. "Did you have a

good time?"

"Great," said Kayla.

They got their car out of the parking garage and started driving to Island Hills on Long Island.

"Oh, I met Dad's girlfriend, Alyssa. She's nice, but I wish you and Dad could work things out," Kayla frowned.

Her mom sighed. "I'm sorry, but we can't get back together. We argued too much."

"Guess what? Amanda got a guinea pig. Can I get a kitten or a guinea pig or a parakeet?" asked Kayla.

"I don't know. I'll have to think about it," smiled her mom.

"Uh-oh, I think we're in a big traffic jam," said Kayla, turning on the radio.

They kept switching from one station to another to the news and to all sorts of music programs on their long drive home.

Chapter Eleven

A SPARKLING DISCOVERY

Vicky and Kayla went to their lockers after ballet class on Thursday afternoon.

Amber came over to them. "My ballet bag is all wet. I think someone wet it on purpose. I was late so I left it on the bench," she said, tears rolling down her cheeks. She handed Kayla her pink ballet bag with white toe shoes on it.

Kayla wrinkled her nose. "Wow, it's sopping wet. Someone may have poured water on it from a water bottle," she said, touching it.

"It was a mean thing to do. It looks like someone wants to scare you and make you dance badly," said Vicky to Amber.

"I'm not going to worry about it. My bag will dry," said Amber.

Kayla took out a plastic bag with the diamond in it from her blue ballet bag with pink toe shoes on it. "Is this diamond from your tiara?" she asked.

"It sure looks like it. Some of the jewels were a little loose," said Amber, holding it. "Where did you find it?"

"It was under Cindy's locker, and we have to keep it for our clue. We're working on the case," said Vicky, taking a sip from her water bottle.

Amber gave back the diamond. "Thanks a lot for helping me," said Amber, and she walked back to her locker.

"Let's wait until everyone leaves and look for clues," said Kayla, after they changed back into their clothes. They waited for several minutes.

"They're all gone now," said Vicky, taking a bite of her raspberry pop tart.

Kayla started shining the flashlight under the lockers, benches and make-up tables as they searched for clues.

"I think I see something," yelled Vicky, kneeling down underneath a make-up table. "It looks like a pink chip from a jewel," she said, picking it up.

"Wow, it looks like it's a chip of a pink sapphire from Amber's tiara. Or maybe it's only a piece of pink glass," said Kayla, peering at it through her magnifying glass.

"It sparkles like a real jewel," said Vicky, looking through the magnifying glass also. "It was under Amy's locker. This could be evidence that Amy stole it."

"The chip could have been moved all over the place, but I think it's a good clue," said Kayla, putting it in a small ziplock bag. "Now we have three bags with clues," she said, holding up the other two bags with the gold barrette and diamond in them.

Just then the janitor came in and started sweeping the floor in the back of the room.

"Let's get out of here," whispered Vicky. They grabbed their things and scooted out the front door.

"We almost got caught," said Kayla, her heart pounding.

Vicky nodded. "Good-bye."

"Bye," said Kayla. She hurried home and got ready to go to the basketball game.

That night, Kayla, Crystal and Marissa walked into the Island Hills Middle School gym.

"Hey. the bleachers are almost completely filled with Leopard fans," said Crystal.

"Yo we're over here, girls," yelled Jamal, from the bleachers.

They sat next to Jamal, Tyrone, Matthew and Jason in the fifth row.

"Kayla, you can sit next to me," smiled Jason.

"Hi," she said, sitting down next to him.

The Leopards, in their white uniforms with navy blue trim, and the Wild Cats, wearing purple and white uniforms from Stoney Creek Middle School, started shooting basketballs to warm up.

Marissa put on her glasses and pointed to the right. "Oh, there's Breanna's parents and her big brother, Travis, and her little brother, Randy."

"Oh yeah," said Kayla. "Sarah's parents and her little sister are sitting behind Breanna's parents."

"The Leopards have improved a lot, but the Wild Cats are the best in the district," said Tyrone.

The whistle blew and the referee threw up the ball for the tip-off. Destiny, the Leopard center and Nia, the Wild Cat center, jumped up to tap it. Destiny jumped higher and tapped the ball to Breanna.

Breanna, wearing number 10 on her jersey, took the ball and dribbled upcourt. She passed to Erin. Erin passed to Isabel. She jumped up, shot, and the ball went through the net.

"Goooo Leopards!" shouted the fans.

At the end of the first quarter, the Wild Cats were leading, 12 to 6.

The Leopards tried to block the Wild Cats. But the Wild Cats had a hot streak and made more baskets than the Leopards.

The Wild Cats were leading 28 to Leopards 20 when the horn blew at halftime.

"You've got to pass more to each other and shoot more baskets," said Coach Taylor to the Leopards in their locker room during their rest time.

"The Leopards have to play better," said Crystal.

"They have to make more baskets," Jamal said.

When the whistle blew, the third quarter began.

Destiny dribbled the ball and passed to Sarah, wearing number 27 on the back of her jersey. As Sarah threw the ball, a Wild Cat hit her arm.

"Two foul shots for number 27," called out the referee, blowing his whistle.

Sarah stood at the foul line and threw the ball. It went through the net. She tossed the ball again, and it went in.

"Hooray, Sarah," chanted the Leopard fans.

Erin took the ball and dribbled toward the basket. "Pass it

to me. I'm open," yelled Lakeysha, waving her hand. Erin bounced the ball to Lakeysha. Lakeysha leaped up, tossed the ball, and it went in.

"Good shot," said Erin.

"Thanks," said Lakeysha. *Now Erin passes to me instead of fighting*, thought Lakeysha.

The Wild Cats were leading the Leopards by eight points at the end of the third quarter.

Coach Taylor started substituting all eleven players to give them all a chance to play during the fourth quarter.

Nia, the Wild Cat center, dribbled the ball downcourt. Breanna stole the ball and passed to Salena who passed to Isabel. She passed to Jennifer. She tossed it, and the ball went spinning around the rim and dropped in.

"Hooray, Jennifer!" yelled the fans.

The Leopards had a hot streak and caught up with the Wild Cats.

Matthew looked at the electric scoreboard. "It's a tie, 54 to 54, with 30 seconds to go," yelled Matthew, biting his lip.

Destiny dribbled the ball and passed to Breanna. She threw the ball 21 feet away. In for two points.

"Hooray, Breanna," yelled the fans.

"Only 11 seconds to go, and the Leopards are leading by two points," shouted Jamal, sitting at the edge of his seat.

"Hold that ball," yelled the Leopard fans, with five seconds to go.

Lakeysha dribbled the ball and passed to Ava. Nia, the

Wild Cat center, stole the ball and threw it 20 feet away. The ball struck the rim and bounced off.

The horn blew loudly.

"The Leopards won, 56 to 54," cried Marissa.

The Leopard fans screamed and cheered.

Jamal, Tyrone, Matthew and Jason slapped each other low and high-fives. Kayla, Crystal and Marissa slapped each other high-fives and hugged each other.

Both teams shook hands with each other.

The Leopards gave each other high-fives. They each shook hands with their coach.

"Great teamwork," said Coach Taylor with a grin.

"Bye, Kayla," said Jason, pushing his wavy brown hair out of his eyes. "I'll see you in school."

"Bye," smiled Kayla.

Kayla, Marissa and Crystal headed for the parking lot. Mrs. Diaz was waiting for them in the car.

They piled into the car and fastened their seat belts.

"How was the game?" Mrs. Diaz wanted to know.

"Great! Leopards won," said Kayla.

"Sarah and Breanna are good basketball players," said Marissa.

"Oh, I forgot to tell you. Amber put up a poster at the ballet school offering a reward for anyone who gives information or finds the tiara," said Kayla.

"That's a good idea! Someone may tell you something important just to get the reward," said Crystal.

Music blared out of the radio during the ride to their homes.

Chapter Twelve

A CLUE AT THE MALL

"Wake up, Kayla," said her mother, coming into her bedroom on Saturday morning. Oliver had a pink ballet slipper in his mouth.

"Give me my slipper," said Kayla. Oliver ran downstairs.

"Ohmigosh, your room is a mess. Look at all the clothes, magazines, papers and CDs piled up on the floor. There's also stuff under your bed," gasped her mother.

"I'm sorry," said Kayla, yawning.

"Clean up this room immediately or else you can't go to the mall today," frowned her mother.

"I don't have time to do it now. I'll do it later," said Kayla.

Her mom sighed. "You have to do it now," she said, leaving the room.

Kayla rolled out of her bed. She picked up her clothes and put them in her closet and dresser drawers. Then she picked up the things that were scattered all over the dark pink carpet.

I'll pick up all the things I have hidden under my bed later. I hope Mom doesn't notice, thought Kayla. She put on her jeans, a violet T-shirt, a white cardigan and her new black and white sneakers.

Then she went into the kitchen and sat down at the table.

"Hi. Did you clean up your room?" asked her mom.

"Yes," said Kayla, stirring butter, raisins and cinnamon in her hot oatmeal.

"Good. Here's the money for you to buy some ski clothes and whatever else you need at the mall," said her mother.

"Thanks Mom," said Kayla, putting the money in her pocketbook.

They heard a car honking. "That must be Marissa," said her mom.

"See you later," said Kayla, putting on her black wool jacket. She ran outside and climbed into the backseat of the car.

After they picked up Sarah and Breanna, Mrs. Diaz drove to the mall and dropped them off in the parking lot.

"Meet me back here at 5:00 this evening. Adiós," said Mrs. Diaz.

"Adiós," chorused the girls.

"Where do you want to go first?" asked Sarah.

"Let's look at clothes," said Marissa. They went into a boutique that had stylish clothes. They went over to a rack filled with all kinds of sweaters. The girls tried on many sweaters. They each chose a sweater they liked best and paid the cashier at the register.

"Where do you want to go next?" asked Sarah.

"I've got to buy ski clothes. I'm going skiing with my father and my cousin during our winter vacation. But I've got to be back for the Nutcracker dress rehearsal and the performance at the end of December after Christmas," explained Kayla.

"Then let's go to the ski store," suggested Breanna.

Kayla led them into a big ski store. She tried on a light blue ski jacket with a hood, filled with goose down feathers.

"It looks pretty on you, and it brings out your blue eyes," said Breanna.

Kayla bought the jacket, matching ski pants, a white wool hat and mittens.

"Let's go to Star's Gift Store that sells cards, earrings, pocketbooks and all kinds of cool stuff," suggested Sarah.

When they went into the store, they started looking at pierced earrings.

"I need some barrettes," said Kayla. She walked to the back of the store, where hairclips, barrettes and hair bands were hanging on hooks.

She saw a girl holding white, round shaped barrettes in her hand.

"Hi, Amy. I'm surprised to see you here," said Kayla.

"Oh, hi," said Amy.

"I like the white round barrettes you're holding," said Kayla.

"They're perfect for Marie's dress. I I I mean for my Sugar Plum Fairy dress," stammered Amy.

"Wouldn't you rather be Marie than the Sugar Plum Fairy?" Kayla asked.

Amy's blue eyes narrowed. "Of course! Then I'd have the

starring role. What did you buy?" she asked, pointing to Kayla's shopping bags.

"I bought ski clothes for my skiing trip I'm going on during my school's winter break," said Kayla.

"You could break your leg or your arm going skiing. Now I'm practicing my ballet steps for the Sugar Plum Fairy. Then I'll practice ballet during my winter vacation in my dance studio in my house," said Amy.

Amy is so serious about ballet, thought Kayla.

"Are you also practicing for Marie?" asked Kayla.

"Yes, because I'm the understudy for Marie," said Amy.

"I just hope Amber gets her tiara back," said Kayla.

Amy nodded her head. "I'm gonna buy the pink sparkly rhinestones and the white barrettes," said Amy, holding them in her hand.

"I'm getting the same white barrettes," said Kayla.

"My mom's waiting for me. Bye," said Amy.

"Bye," Kayla said.

Kayla watched Amy pay the cashier for the barrettes. Then she saw Amy and Amy's mother leave the store.

Amy goofed when she said she wanted to buy the white barrettes for Marie. This is a new clue, thought Kayla.

Breanna, Sarah and Marissa bought sterling silver pierced earrings, and Kayla bought the barrettes.

They wandered around the mall going in and out of stores. "We'd better eat our lunch now cuz it's getting late," said Breanna.

The girls went into a restaurant and sat down in a booth. They gave a waitress their order.

"Oh, I saw Amy buying barrettes today. She goofed and said she was buying these white barrettes to wear for Marie's dress. Then she quickly said she's buying them for the Sugar Plum Fairy's dress. We have a lot of evidence that proves that Amy wants to be Marie so much that she may do anything to mess up Amber," explained Kayla.

"The thief could be someone you least suspect. You have to get real proof before you accuse anyone," Sarah said.

"That's what Vicky and I are working on," said Kayla.

"Anyway, what are all of you doing during our winter break?" asked Sarah, taking a bite into her grilled cheese sandwich.

"My family celebrates Christmas and Kwanza which both come at the end of December," said Breanna.

"What's Kwanza?" asked Marissa.

"It's a holiday that celebrates our African heritage," said Breanna.

"How do you celebrate it?" asked Marissa, pouring ketchup over her French fries.

"We place seven candles in the kinara, a Kwanza candle-holder. We light one candle each night to celebrate one of the seven principles, until all seven candles are burning on the last night. My favorite night is when my family and my aunts, uncles and cousins go to my grandparent's house for a karamu, a yummy feast. Tyrone and Jamal told me that they also celebrate Kwanza," said Breanna.

"Cool!" said Marissa. "I can't wait until Christmas because my grandparents are visiting us from Peru in South America."

"Sarah, are you doing anything special?" asked Kayla.

"My family celebrates Chanukah which comes some time in December and lasts for eight days. We use a special candle holder, called a menorah. On the first night we light one candle with a match. By the last night, all eight candles are lit," explained Sarah.

"Do you get presents?" asked Breanna.

Sarah nodded. "My sister, Rachel, who's eight and I get presents from our parents and our grandparents. But we don't get presents every night. We're also going to a Chanukah party at our temple," she said.

"By the way, a new horror movie is coming out soon. My mom said she'll drive us there," said Breanna.

"Cool! Why don't we invite boys," said Marissa.

"Good idea!" said Kayla.

"It's almost 5:00. We have to meet my mother in the parking lot," said Marissa.

"Thank you," said the waitress, giving each girl a separate check.

Each girl left a tip and paid the cashier.

"Hola girls," said Mrs. Diaz.

"Hi," chorused the girls, scrambling into the car.

"What did you buy?" asked Mrs. Diaz.

"I bought ski clothes for my ski trip," said Kayla, showing them to her.

"We used to go skiing when we lived in Pennsylvania," said Mrs. Diaz as she was driving the girls to their homes.

"I liked to ski, but it was hard to do. I fell a lot in the snow," Marissa laughed.

"I can't wait to go to the Princess and the Pirates play next week. It's going to be so exciting seeing Kayla and Marissa acting on the stage," said Breanna.

"All our friends are coming," added Sarah.

"I hope we don't mess up our lines," Kayla said.

"Just make-believe that you didn't goof," Breanna said.

They all laughed.

Chapter Thirteen

PRINCESS AND THE PIRATES' DRESS REHEARSAL

Mr. Glasser stood on the stage of the auditorium on Friday afternoon. "We've had many rehearsals, even during your recesses. This dress rehearsal is our last chance to practice before our show tomorrow night. Ray Jones, the writer of this play, will be coming to see our show."

"Hooray," yelled out some of the students.

The girls and boys who were stagehands hung up a huge painting of a palace. They carried in the throne they made out of wood and had painted it gold.

"Everybody in Act 1, Scene 1 go onstage now," yelled Mr. Glasser.

Shannon as Queen Anne wore a metal gold crown with jewels on it and a long, orange dress. Frank as the king, wore a metal gold crown and a long, purple velvet robe. They sat at the throne.

Shannon started saying her lines.

Then Kayla, wearing a long, blue satin dress and a small plastic gold crown on her head, started speaking. But she stopped in the middle of a line. "I I can't remember my lines," she stammered.

Shannon rolled her hazel eyes. "I told you I should have

gotten the part as the princess," she yelled.

"Shannon, be quiet!" said Mrs. Melon.

"Kayla, the king tells you he's arranging a marriage for you. It's with the rich Count Ralph now that you're 18 years old. And you tell him you want to marry a man you fall in love with," said Mr. Glasser.

"I remember now," said Kayla, saying her lines.

Count Ralph, played by Eddie, wore a long green shirt and yellow pants. "I'm so glad to meet you," he said, stepping on Kayla's foot.

"Ouch," said Kayla.

"I'm sorry," said Eddie, starting to giggle.

"Eddie, this is no joke," said Mrs. Melon.

"That was pretty good. Everyone in Scene 2, go backstage now," Mr. Glasser said.

The stagehands changed the Scenery to a huge painting of the deep blue sea. They dragged in the big wood ship that was painted brown.

Kayla and her governess, Hilda, played by Crystal, were taking a walk by the sea. Crystal wore a gray wig, a silver dress and green beads.

"My mom loaned me her jade necklace. Many Chinese people believe that jade is good luck," whispered Crystal to Kayla.

"It's beautiful," said Kayla.

The eight pirates wore T-shirts and bright colored scarves on their heads. They grabbed Princess Emma and dragged her to their big ship. "Ouch, you're hurting my arm," said Kayla.

The stagehands changed the scenery to the palace.

Governess Hilda ran back to the palace. "The princess has been kidnapped by pirates," she screamed. They told me they want silver and gold and jewels, or else the princess will never come back."

"Good, Crystal," said Mr. Glasser.

Queen Anne, Meg and Princess Emma's three ladies-in-waiting, Anna, Ella and Eva, all started crying.

"We've got to save Princess Emma," yelled King Edward.

Stephanie as Anna, Julie as Ella, and Grace as Eva wore gold necklaces and long dresses.

The stagehands put up a painting of a forest.

Seven boy servants, wearing long shirts over their pants, put up posters on cardboard trees offering a reward for anyone who can save the princess.

The poster said:

A handsome reward of silver, gold and jewels will be granted for the brave men that rescue princess Emma from Captain Red Fox and his pirates.

Bring her back to Queen Anne and King Edward alive.

Then the stagehands changed the scenery to the ocean painting. They pushed in a small gray wood ship for Act 1, Scene 3.

"This is the scene when George, the handsome, young

blacksmith and sword maker and his three friends, who are also sword makers, get a boat to rescue the princess," said Mr. Glasser.

George, played by Andrew, Brian, played by Joe, James played by Jim, and Ted, played by Greg got on a small wood ship. They wore long shirts and pants.

When they finished Scene 3, the stagehands replaced the smaller wood ship for Captain Red Fox's larger wood ship.

"Everyone in Scene 4, onstage now," called out Mr. Glasser. "By the way, I want to thank Joe's father for helping the stagehands make the throne and the ships out of wood cartons. He's a great carpenter."

Everyone started clapping their hands.

Captain Red Fox, played by Matthew, wore a red cloak, black pointed boots and a black hat on top of his brown, curly hair. The captain's three meanest pirates, Snuff, played by Jamal, Hammer Head, played by Zackery, and Jake as Hawk Eye, and Kayla got on the huge wood ship.

"Your father, King Edward, better give us the jewels or you'll be thrown overboard," yelled Captain Red Fox.

Kayla made believe she was crying. "Please let me go home."

"You're doing very well so far. Take a twenty minute break," called out Mr. Glasser.

The stagehands added the smaller wood ship near the big wood ship for Act 2, Scene 1.

After the break, the pirates, George, and the three other

sword makers, got onstage carrying their long, pointed swords made of plastic.

Then the pirates and sword makers started dueling with their swords.

Captain Red Fox and George clashed swords.

"Ow, you scratched my arm," groaned Andrew, pointing his sword at the captain's chin.

Matthew's brown eyes narrowed. "Ouch, you scratched my chin."

Then Hammer Head and Brian clashed swords.

"You poked my neck," yelled Zackery to Joe.
They threw down their swords and started punching each other.

"Stop it," yelled Mr. Glasser.

Everyone onstage stood still.

"You have to always stay in the character you're playing," frowned Mr. Glasser.

"This is only make-believe. Be careful," added Mrs. Melon. "Let's continue now."

George and his friends threw Captain Red Fox and the pirates overboard.

The stagehands quickly moved the big ship backstage.

Then Kayla, George, Brian, James and Ted got into the small ship. George told Princess Emma he loved her on the ship. All of a sudden there was a big thunderstorm. A stagehand put a CD of a thunderstorm in the stereo. The stagelights dimmed and flickered on and off for lightning and a fan blew strips of cellophane paper onstage to simulate a thunderstorm.

"Very good," said Mr. Glasser to the stagehands.

"Now for the last scene of Act 2," called out Mrs. Melon.

The stagehands carried small tables and chairs on the stage. Then they hung up paintings and decorations for the grand ballroom in the palace.

Count Ralph and Princess Emma began dancing to slow music playing on the stereo.

Anna, Ella and Eva danced with the rich young lords.

A young lord, played by Alex, was dancing too fast with Princess Emma's younger sister Meg, played by Marissa.

"Slow down," yelled Marissa, tripping on her long pink dress.

George stood on his knees in front of Kayla and asked her to marry him. Count Ralph got in the way and bumped into George. George fell on the floor.

Andrew's blue eyes narrowed. "Watch out," he yelled.

"Sorry," frowned Eddie.

"Kayla, it's your turn to speak," said Mrs. Melon.

"Umm, I I I forgot my lines," stammered Kayla.

Shannon made a nasty face at Kayla.

"It's when you tell your father you're in love with George, and that he wants to marry you," said Mrs. Melon.

"Oh yeah, thanks," said Kayla, saying her lines.

When they finished rehearsing, Mr. Glasser stood on the stage.

Everyone came to the front and looked up at him.

"The dress rehearsal was good. But all of you have to

practice your lines again. If you forget your lines during the performance think of the scene you're in. Also, someone will be in the wings to give you verbal cues. Get a good night's sleep. Put on your costumes and make-up at home. Be back at the auditorium at 6:00 tomorrow night. The show starts at 8:00," Mr. Glasser said.

Everyone hurried out of the auditorium.

"Hi," said Marissa and Kayla, climbing into Mrs. Diaz's car.

"I'm so nervous," said Kayla.

"I'm sure you girls will do great in the play," said Mrs. Diaz, driving to Kayla's house.

When Kayla opened the front door of her house, Oliver barked and jumped up on her. She patted his head and walked into the kitchen.

"Hi, Grandma," said Kayla.

"Hello, dinner's almost ready," said her grandma, taking the meatloaf out of the oven. "Your mom's coming home late. She has to go to an editor's meeting."

"Oh, okay," said Kayla.

"Tomorrow night is your big performance," said her grandma.

Kayla started biting her fingernails. "I'm getting nervous. What if I forget my lines?"

Her grandma sighed. "You've been rehearsing almost every night. You're just getting a little stage fright."

"Grandma, will you practice with me tonight?" asked

Kayla.

Grandma smiled. "Why not, I've been doing it for several weeks."

After dinner, Kayla and her grandmother rehearsed the play together in the living room.

Kayla laughed. "Grandma, you're so funny when you read the other characters in the play. You even sound like George."

"That's because I read picture books to the little children as a part-time librarian. Your grandpa would be so proud of you. I miss him so much, but I have my memories," said Grandma.

"I miss him, also," said Kayla.

She hurried to her bedroom and did her science and math homework. Looking in the mirror above her dresser, Kayla practiced her lines over and over again. *I guess I know my lines pretty well. I only had to look at the script a few times. But sometimes my mind goes blank. Oh, well, I'll just do my best,* thought Kayla.

Chapter Fourteen

SHOW TIME

Racing into the auditorium of her school, Kayla hurried backstage. It was 6:00 on Saturday night. She was dressed in her blue dress, gold pointed shoes and wore a gold necklace. She had already put on her make-up in her house.

"Everyone should all be in their costumes. Go over your lines once more. This is your last chance before the show," Mr. Glasser called out.

Some of the students went into rooms backstage to practice their parts. Matthew, Andrew and Kayla kept reading their scripts over and over to themselves in one of the small rooms.

I think I've practiced enough. I hope I don't forget my lines, Kayla was thinking.

Marissa and Kayla peeked through the dark green, satin curtains from the left wing.

"A lot of people are coming into the auditorium now. Tyler, Shari, David, Hailey and Chelsea are ushers. They're handing out the programs," Marissa said, wearing her eyeglasses. "I don't need to wear my eyeglasses during the play," she explained.

"Oh, I see my mom, Dad and my grandmother sitting in the second row. I think that man with the bushy mustache is Ray Jones, the playwright of our play. He's sitting in the first row," said Kayla excitedly.

"There's a lot of sixth, seventh and eighth grade students coming in now," Marissa said. "And there's my mother, father and José in the first row."

"Oh look. Sarah, Breanna, Tyrone, Jason and Anthony are going into the third row now," said Kayla, bouncing up and down.

"Hi," said Andrew, coming over to them. "Hey, my mom and dad and my little sister, Brooke, are sitting in the fourth row," he said, looking at the audience.

"Our play will be starting shortly. All the actors in Act 1, take your places onstage," said Mrs. Melon, from backstage. "Everyone else, sit in a room backstage, until we call you."

The house lights dimmed. Billy pulled open the curtains. The bright stage lights went on.

First the king and queen spoke to the princess.

Then it was Kayla's turn to speak. She glanced at the audience and started to freeze. When she opened her mouth, nothing came out. *I feel dizzy*, she thought. Kayla took a deep breath and started speaking softly.

Then there was complete silence. *I forgot my lines*, thought Andrew.

Kayla started speaking, covering up for him.

Andrew took a deep breath. He started saying his lines

too fast, but they made it through the first scene.

During Scene 2, the pirates started pulling Kayla very hard to the ship. Kayla fell on the floor. Captain Red Fox quickly picked her up.

The audience laughed loudly.

Uh-oh, I forgot my lines, thought Kayla when it was her turn to speak. Then there was a long silence.

Standing off stage, Billy gave Kayla a verbal cue.

I remember, she thought, saying her lines loud and clear.

Everything was going smoothly until the big wood ship collided with the small wood ship. The small wood ship tipped over. Joe quickly picked it up.

Then the captain and the pirates and George and the sword makers started fighting with each other with their swords.

Matthew's sword flew off the stage. Jason stood up in the audience and threw it back to Matthew. When Matthew caught it, the audience laughed.

Brian poked his sword into Snuff's chest.

"Ouch," said Jamal to Joe. They started hitting each other's swords very hard. Jamal lost his balance and fell on the floor.

When Captain Red Fox and the pirates were thrown overboard, the audience cheered. The pirates made believe they were swimming in the ocean as they ran off the stage.

King Edward started taking out the jewels and coins from the chest to give to George and his three friends. The chest tipped over, and the jewels and coins fell on the floor. Everyone onstage started picking them up while people in the audience howled with laughter.

During the last scene, the ladies-in-waiting danced with the lords to the music. Count Ralph was dancing with Princess Emma. Suddenly, Count Ralph tripped on jewels that were laying on the floor. Eddie fell down on his back. He slowly got up. Kayla, Julie and Grace started giggling.

"Eddie wasn't supposed to fall," said Tyrone to Jason and Anthony, sitting in the audience. They burst out laughing.

Alex started whirling Marissa around very fast as they were dancing. Marissa tripped. She fell down and her dress went up. Alex quickly pulled her up, and they started to dance again.

I'm so embarrassed. I hope they think it's part of the act, thought Marissa.

Kayla's gold plastic crown fell off, and she quickly put it back on. *I hope we can find Amber's tiara, so she can wear it at the ballet,* thought Kayla.

Everyone cheered when King Edward told George that he could marry Princess Emma. "The queen and I will make all the arrangements for the wedding," said King Edward.

Kayla and Andrew started to laugh but put their hands over their mouths.

"This is some happy ending," said Breanna to Sarah in the audience.

When the last scene ended, the curtains closed. Everyone

hurried backstage. "I want all the main characters to get ready to take their bows first," said Mr. Glasser.

Then Billy pulled open the curtains.

One at a time, the king, queen, George, Count Ralph, Captain Red Fox, Meg, Hilda, James, Ted, Brian, Snuff, Hammer Head and Hawk Eye came onstage. The girls curtsied and the boys bowed to the audience. The audience clapped and cheered.

When Kayla came onstage, the audience stood up and applauded and yelled, "Bravo!"

Kayla took a deep curtsy and smiled.

Then the entire cast lined up across the stage. The audience applauded wildly. They stood up and yelled, "Bravo, bravo!"

Then the curtains closed for the last time.

Mr. Glasser and the man with the bushy mustache came backstage. "I'd like you to meet Ray Jones, our playwright," announced Mr. Glaser.

"You all did a wonderful job," said Ray Jones.

"You were great. I'm very proud of all of you," Mr. Glasser beamed.

"Everything worked out just fine!" Mrs. Melon said.

The actors left the stage and looked for their parents and relatives in the auditorium. Kayla rushed over to her parents and her grandma.

"You were the best princess," Grandma said, her blue-gray eyes glowing.

"You have a flair for acting. I was a good actor in some of my school plays," smiled Kayla's father.

"Daddy, may I take acting lessons?" Kayla asked.

"Of course you can," said her father.

"That's a wonderful idea," said her mother.

Breanna, Sarah, Tyrone, Anthony, and Jason came over to Kayla.

"You were great," said Breanna as she and Sarah hugged her.

"You were terrific," said Jason, shaking her hand.

Tyrone and Anthony nodded. "Yeah," they agreed.

"Thank you," beamed Kayla.

Then her friends left.

Marissa came over to Kayla. "My mother wants to take us to the cast party now," said Marissa.

"Okay," said Kayla.

Kayla said good-bye to her mom, Dad and Grandma. She and Marissa went over to Marissa's parents.

"I'm glad to meet you. You were great as Princess Emma," said Mr. Diaz, peering through his silver wire-framed eyeglasses.

"Thank you," said Kayla.

Mr. Diaz turned to Marissa and José. "I'll see you next weekend." He hugged them and walked away.

"Your father is so nice," said Kayla.

"Yeah, but I wish I could see him more. He works long hours cuz he's a computer programmer," said Marissa.

Mrs. Diaz, José, Marissa and Kayla climbed into the silver car.

Mrs. Diaz started driving to Crystal's house.

"Kayla, you acted like a real princess," said Mrs. Diaz.

"Kayla, you were good," José chimed in.

"Gracias, thank you. I'm glad you thought I acted well, but I forgot my lines a few times," Kayla admitted.

"I tripped and fell on the floor," added Marissa.

"Actors sometimes make mistakes. I'm so proud of both of you," beamed Mrs. Diaz.

"Adiós," Marissa and Kayla said when they reached Crystal's house.

Marissa rang the doorbell. Crystal opened the front door, still wearing her gray wig and a long silver dress.

"Hi, I'm glad you could come to my cast party," said Crystal.

They followed Crystal downstairs.

"Wow, your basement is huge," said Kayla.

"That's because I live in a ranch house," said Crystal.

Almost everyone in the drama class were already there.

Kayla and Marissa walked over to a long table filled with soda, a huge bowl of yellow lemonade and cookies and cakes. Crystal's grandmother, wearing a red silk Chinese dress, put a big plate of cheese and crackers on the table.

"Everyone's still wearing their costumes," said Kayla to Marissa.

"Hi, Princess Emma and Meg," said Matthew, biting into

a piece of chocolate layer cake. He pointed his sword at two pirates, Jake and Zackery.

The pirates pointed their swords back at Matthew.

"Hey governess Hilda, do you want to dance?" asked Matthew.

Crystal and Matthew started doing a fast dance with music blasting from the stereo. When Crystal's wig fell off, they both laughed.

Andrew went over to the refreshments and started eating a lot of cookies.

"Hey, Meg, would you like to dance?" asked Andrew.

"Yes, George," said Marissa, and they went to the part of the room where everyone was dancing.

Joe, one of the sword makers, came over to Kayla.

"Would you like to dance?"

"Okay," said Kayla, and they started to dance.

"Look at Shannon dancing with Frank. She's showing off as usual," said Kayla to Joe.

Just then, Shannon stared at Kayla. "I would have been a better Princess Emma than you," she said.

Kayla rolled her eyes. "Everybody thought I was very good."

"Whatever," said Shannon as she and Frank went over to the refreshments.

"I'm glad you got to be Princess Emma instead of Shannon," said Joe. "You were very good."

"Thank you," said Kayla with a smile.

When the song ended, Kayla sat next to Marissa and a group of girls and boys, sitting in a circle.

"C'mon Jamal. Please rap for us," called out Eddie.

"Okay, sure why not," muttered Jamal.

Crystal turned the music off and handed Eddie a drum. Jamal rapped and danced, while Eddie beat on the drum with his hands. Everyone clapped their hands when they finished.

"Marissa, your mom is outside, waiting in the car," said Crystal.

"Thank you for having the party," Marissa said.

"Bye," they said, leaving her house.

Mrs. Diaz and José were sitting in the front seat as Marissa and Kayla got in the backseat of the car.

"So how was the cast party?" asked Mrs. Diaz, driving to Kayla's home.

"We had a good time," said Marissa.

"I wish I could be Captain Red Fox or a pirate and fight with a sword," said José.

"You'd make a great pirate. I'll buy you a plastic sword," said Mrs. Diaz.

"Can I also get a pirate costume?" José asked.

"Of course!" said Mrs. Diaz.

"Yipee," José said.

They burst out laughing.

"I can't wait to go to the horror movie with our friends," Marissa said, her brown eyes widening.

"Yeah. I'm getting the chills just thinking about it," Kayla said.

When they parked in front of Kayla's house, Marissa said, "Hasta luego, see you later."

"Adiós amigos," Kayla said.

"Adiós," Mrs. Diaz, José and Marissa said, waving good-bye.

Chapter Fifteen

MUMMIES IN A PARADE

The next Saturday afternoon , Mrs. Williams was driving Sarah, Kayla, Marissa and Breanna to the movies.

"Have a good time, girls," said Mrs. Williams, driving into the parking lot.

"Thank you," said the girls. They headed to the movie theater.

"Hi," said the girls to the boys, getting on the line in front of Matthew, Anthony, Tyrone and Jason.

"I'll get us eight seats together before the theater fills up," said Jason.

"And we'll buy the food and drinks," said Tyrone.

They carried popcorn, candy and soda into the dark theater.

"Over here," called out Jason.

"Who do you want to sit next to?" asked Matthew.

"It doesn't make a difference. Hurry up and sit down. The coming attractions are coming on soon," said Anthony.

When they scrambled into the seats, Sarah fell on Matthew's lap.

"Oops, sorry," she said.

Kayla sat between Sarah and Marissa.

"I know you want to sit next to Jason," teased Marissa, putting on her eyeglasses.

Marissa and Kayla exchanged seats. "Hiya," Kayla said, sitting next to Jason.

"Hi," said Jason.

"Breanna is sitting next to Tyrone, just as she wanted to," giggled Marissa.

Then the coming attractions started.

The movie finally began. A gigantic mummy, in white bandages, from head to toe, with two small black eyes, escaped from his grave in a cemetery.

Matthew started throwing popcorn at the girls. Kayla and Marissa threw popcorn back at him.

"Stop it," said Sarah.

A man, wearing an ugly, green monster mask started following a girl and a boy walking in a parking lot. The masked man grabbed the girl with his sharp, long nails. Breanna, Marissa and Kayla put their hands over their eyes.

"Scaredy cats," said Matthew.

"Don't be scared," whispered Jason to Kayla, tugging on her ponytail.

"Please pass the popcorn and candy," whispered Matthew. Sarah gave him the bucket and junior mints.

The mummy appeared and started fighting with the masked man. The mummy kept reappearing again and again every time the green masked man attacked someone.

"The mummy looks scary, but he's really not a bad guy," whispered Jason to Kayla.

"He seems okay," said Kayla.

The mummy tried pulling the green mask off the man, when the masked man squeezed a woman's neck in a forest. The mask didn't come off. The masked man's hands turned into long, sharp claws.

"Uh-oh, the man with the mask is a real monster," remarked Tyrone.

The mummy and the masked man started fighting on a bridge. The mummy threw the monster into the river. Then many other mummies came out of their graves. They started marching around the town.

"It looks like the mummies are marching in a parade," laughed Anthony.

Thunder crashed and rain came pouring down. The mummies walked stiffly and slowly to the cemetery, scrambling back into their graves.

Suddenly the green monster poked his head out of the water in the river.

"Hey, the green monster is still alive. That was a cool ending," said Matthew.

"The movie was more like a comedy than a horror movie," Anthony said.

"I think the mummy was cute, and he was a real hero," said Marissa.

After they left the movie theater, they walked over to the

Icy Palace ice cream parlor. They sat down in a big booth and ordered ice cream from the waiter.

The waiter gave Matthew a super deluxe sundae with six scoops of ice cream, smothered with pecans, chocolate syrup and whipped cream.

"Yuck, that's too much ice cream," said Sarah.

"It's not too much for me," laughed Matthew.

"Would you like to come to our basketball game on Monday night?" asked Tyrone.

Anthony's blue eyes lit up. "It's going to be a tough game. The Sharks are playing against the Jaguars."

"I'll go," said Matthew. The others nodded their heads yes.

"How's your detective work going?" asked Marissa.

Kayla shrugged. "Okay, but I feel Vicky and I are going around in circles. We got more clues, but we haven't any real proof."

"Basketball is really hard work and we have to practice three times a week. I think taking ballet lessons and playing detective is a lot easier," said Breanna, rolling her dark brown eyes.

"Yeah, I agree," said Sarah.

Kayla shook her head. "Ballet is harder, and you have to go two or three times a week in the most advanced classes. But I think being a detective is the most difficult of all."

"Strutting up on your toes and snooping around is easier than playing basketball," Tyrone said.

"I have an idea. Let's make a bet," said Breanna to Kayla. "If you find the tiara in time for Amber to wear it at the Nutcracker, you win the bet. Sarah and I will treat you at the ice cream parlor. However, if the Leopards get into the playoffs, Sarah and I also win the bet, and you have to treat us to ice cream."

"What if we both win?" asked Kayla.

"Then we get to go to the ice cream parlor two times," Sarah said.

"I don't think it's fair that Kayla has to treat both Breanna and Sarah," said Marissa.

"If Kayla wins, we'll treat her to a hamburger and ice cream," declared Sarah.

"Can I go with you to the ice cream parlor if you win the bets?" asked Marissa.

"Yes," said Sarah, Breanna and Kayla in unison.

"I think the bet is wack," said Matthew.

"I think it's funny," said Tyrone.

The waiter handed Matthew the check. "Phew, it's a lot of money." He told each of them how much they owed, and they gave it to him. Then Matthew paid the cashier.

Breanna called her mother on her cell phone to tell her to pick them up.

They starting walking back to the parking lot of the movie theater. "Hey, Kayla and Breanna. Are both of you going ice skating with Jason and me tomorrow?" asked Tyrone.

"Yes, we'll meet you at the ice skating rink tomorrow at

1:30 in the afternoon," said Breanna.

Kayla nodded her head. "I'm going."

Anthony's father drove into the parking lot. "Good-bye," said the boys, piling into the car and drove off.

"Oh, here comes my mother," said Breanna.

They all scrambled into the vanilla white minivan.

"How was the movie?" Mrs. Williams asked.

"Pretty creepy," said Marissa.

"It was cool and kind of scary," said Sarah.

"The boys laughed a lot. They thought it was funny," Kayla said.

"I'm glad all of you enjoyed the movie," laughed Mrs. Williams, driving the girls to their houses.

Breanna turned on music on the radio. The girls hummed and sang along to songs they all knew.

Chapter Sixteen

DOUBLE DATE-DOUBLE DUTCH

I t was brisk and sunny the next day as Kayla and Breanna rode their bicycles to the ice skating rink. Kayla wore jeans and a short, white jacket, and Breanna wore a short silver jacket and jeans.

The girls parked their bicycles in the bicycle rack next to Tyrone and Jason's bikes in the parking lot outside of the ice skating rink.

"Hi," said Jason and Tyrone. They were wearing short black jackets and blue jeans.

"I brought my own skates," smiled Breanna.

Tyrone, Jason and Kayla rented their skates, and they put them on. Then they headed for the rink.

They started skating on the huge outdoor ice skating rink. Kayla started slipping and quickly held onto the metal railing. Jason and Breanna glided on the ice. Tyrone started skating fast and fell.

"How long have you been skating?" asked Breanna.

Tyrone picked himself up. "Not long. I've gone a few times with my little brother. I didn't ice skate when I used to live in South Carolina where it's hot all year," Tyrone explained. Then he tightened the laces on his black ice skates.

"I started skating when I was six years old and I've had lessons for three years," said Breanna. Tyrone and Breanna held hands as they skated around the rink.

Jason skated over to Kayla, who was holding onto the railing. "You'll need to let go of the rail," he said.

"I can't skate," said Kayla.

"You just need to practice a lot," said Jason.

"Hi," said Tyrone and Breanna, skating over to Kayla and Jason.

They watched Breanna skate backwards as her white skates sparkled on the ice in the sun. Then she started spinning around and turning on the ice to the music playing over the loudspeaker.

Kayla, Jason and Tyrone clapped their hands. "Wow, I wish I could skate like that," said Jason.

Kayla, Jason, Breanna and Tyrone started skating together, holding each other's hands. Kayla slipped and bumped into Jason. Then Jason bumped into Breanna. They collided into each other, and they all fell on the hard ice. They burst out laughing.

"Let's skate by ourselves for a while," said Breanna.

"Hey Kayla, you're skating without holding the railing," Jason called out.

Kayla looked up. "Oops," she said, falling on her knees.

Jason skated over to Kayla. They started skating very slowly together, holding hands.

"This is fun," said Kayla.

"You're skating much better now," said Jason.

Tyrone and Breanna skated over to Kayla. "Hey, Kayla, your teeth are chattering," said Tyrone.

"I'm getting a little cold," said Kayla.

"Me too," said Breanna.

"Let's stop now. We've been skating for over two hours," said Tyrone, checking his watch.

They walked into a diner across the street. Jason sat next to Kayla and Tyrone sat next to Breanna in a booth. They gave their order to the waitress, and she wrote it down on one check.

"I love to ice skate. I wish I could become a professional ice skater or a pro basketball player," said Breanna, munching on a French fried potato.

"I wanna be a pro basketball player," said Tyrone, taking a bite of his hamburger.

"My little brother and I play baseball in Little League. Maybe I could be a pro baseball player or a fireman like my dad," said Jason.

Kayla sighed. "I'm not sure what I want to be. For now, I have to focus on getting Amber's tiara back."

"Why are you playing detective?" asked Tyrone.

"I think what happened to Amber is wrong. It is not fair that someone else has the tiara. Vicky and I want to catch the thief," said Kayla.

"That's nice of you," said Breanna.

"Here's your check," said the waitress, placing it on the table. "Thank you."

"I'll figure out how much each of you have to pay," said Tyrone.

"That's called double dutch. Everyone each pays for themselves," said Jason.

They all started laughing. Kayla, Jason and Breanna gave Tyrone the money they owed.

"Don't forget to leave the tip," said Breanna.

They all put down money for the tip. Tyrone paid the cashier.

They walked to the bicycle rack outside of the ice skating rink.

"I had a great time," said Jason.

"Me too," smiled Kayla as her heart started beating fast.

"I'll see you in school," said Jason with a grin.

Tyrone and Jason climbed on their bikes and put on their helmets. "Bye," they called as they rode away.

"Bye," said the girls.

Breanna and Kayla climbed on their bikes and put on their helmets.

"We had a lot of fun," said Kayla. "Jason was really nice to me when we were skating."

"And Tyrone was so funny," laughed Breanna. "Let's take the short cut home the back way, around all the houses and those huge mansions."

"Okay," said Kayla as they rode their bikes out of the parking lot and down a long, narrow street.

Chapter Seventeen

SHARKS' AND JAGUARS' FIERCE BASKETBALL GAME

"Hi, Kayla," said Vicky, coming over to her at the barre in ballet class on Monday afternoon.

"Hi, I have to talk to you after class about a new clue," said Kayla.

"Come to the centre now," said Madame Sofia. The students did several ballet steps without the barre. "Find something to spot on and start doing pirouettes," she said to everyone.

Kayla spotted by looking at a mark on the wall and started spinning and turning. All of a sudden, Kayla felt someone push her with their hands on her back. "Oops," she mumbled, falling.

"Are you alright?" Tamara asked.

"Ow, I hurt my wrist," mumbled Kayla, getting up. She looked around, but no one was near her. *Someone pushed me. It wasn't an accident*, she thought.

After class, Kayla and Vicky changed into their clothes and then sat on the bench next to their lockers.

"I think someone pushed me as I was doing a pirouette in class today," whispered Kayla.

"Maybe someone bumped into you by accident," said

Vicky.

Kayla shook her head. "Someone pushed me real hard. My wrist still hurts a little."

"Whoever did it may be giving us a warning to stop snooping around. The person may try to hurt one of us again. We'd better be more alert from now on," Vicky said, frowning.

Kayla nodded. "Oh, I got another clue when I saw Amy at a store at the mall. She goofed when she said she was buying white barrettes to wear for Marie which proves that she really thinks she's going to be Marie," she said softly.

"I've been talking to my dad about our mystery. He told me that some people steal things and then return it in order to look like a hero," whispered Vicky.

Kayla nodded. "Wow, I didn't think of that. The person may even want a reward from Amber for returning it like a metal for bravery. Who do you think needs to be a big hero?" asked Kayla.

"Umm, I think Nicole, Dylan or maybe Cindy would want to look like heroes to everyone," laughed Vicky.

Kayla wrote down their names with the motive to be a hero in her detective notebook. "Oh, by the way, do you want to go to the Artifact Museum on Long Island on Saturday?" asked Kayla. "It has a big jewel collection, and it had a jewel robbery there a few years ago."

"I'll ask my mom and call you. Bye," said Vicky, and she left.

A few minuets later, Kayla walked out the front door. *Oh,*

there's Amy and Julien standing under the big oak tree. I want to find out what they're talking about, thought Kayla.

She quickly hid behind the bushes very close to them and tried to listen to what they were saying. Cars kept honking. She could only hear a little bit of their conversation.

Amy said, "tiara."

Then Julien said, "stupid. On the bench."

Then a car honked.

Then Amy uttered, "in the garage."

Julien said, "a lot of money."

It got so noisy outside, Kayla couldn't hear what they were saying anymore. Then Amy and Julien started laughing. Just then, Amy looked over at the bushes where Kayla was hiding.

Oh, no, maybe Amy saw me, Kayla thought, her heart pounding.

Then Amy and Julien started walking away from the school and down the street.

Maybe they stole the tiara and hid it in the garage. I'm sure they're going to their house. I'll follow them. Then I'll try to sneak into their garage and look for the tiara, thought Kayla.

Kayla ran on the tips of her sneakers after Julien and Amy. When they stopped at a red light, she hid behind a tree. When the light turned green, Kayla crossed the street and followed them down a long, winding road. Suddenly, Julien and Amy stopped abruptly and turned around. Kayla ducked behind a mailbox.

Could they have seen me? Do they think I'm following them, wondered Kayla, her heart racing.

Then Julien and Amy walked down the road. Kayla followed them but stayed far behind them. Julien and Amy stopped at another red light. When the light turned green, they crossed the street with many other people. When Kayla got to the light, it turned red again. When it turned green, she looked across the street, but Julien and Amy were gone.

Oh, I lost them, she thought, and Kayla ran all the way to her house.

"Kayla, where have you been?" asked her grandma as she walked into the den. Oliver was barking and wagging his tail.

"I'm sorry I'm late. I was delayed at ballet school," said Kayla. *I can't tell her why I'm really late*, she thought.

"Dinner is ready. Your mom's coming home late," said her grandma.

"Oh, I forgot. I'm going to the basketball game tonight. I'm glad Breanna's late. Her mother is driving us there," said Kayla.

Kayla changed into a turquoise long-sleeved V-neck sweater and jeans. She put on pink lip gloss.

She was eating her dinner when she heard a car honking. Oliver started barking.

"It's Mrs. William's car," said her grandma, peeking out the front window.

"See you later, Grandma," said Kayla. She grabbed an

apple as she ran out the door.

It was 7:00 that night when Kayla, Sarah, Marissa and Breanna hurried into the Island Hills Middle School gym.

"Wow, what a huge crowd," said Sarah.

"Yo girls, we're up here," yelled Jamal, from the fourth row in the bleachers.

The girls bounded up the narrow stairs and sat down next to Jamal, Andrew and Jason.

"Kayla, I saved you a seat," said Jason. He was wearing a yellow long-sleeved shirt and khaki pants.

Kayla sat next to Jason. "Thanks," she said with a smile. *Jason really looks cute*, thought Kayla.

"Hi," said Lakeysha and Jennifer, running up the stairs. They sat down next to Sarah and Breanna.

"Hi, we're glad you came to the game," said Sarah.

The Sharks, wearing white, trimmed with navy blue uniforms, and the Jaguars, from Yorktown Middle School, wearing gold and black uniforms, just finished practicing taking shots at the basket.

"This should be some fierce game. Both teams are really good," said Jamal.

"Too bad you didn't make the team," said Matthew to Jamal, biting into a Snicker's candy bar.

Jamal shrugged. "It was mad hard to get on the team, and I'm kind of short. But I'm real fast. Maybe I'll make it next year."

The referee blew his whistle and threw up the ball.

Dwayne, the very tall Shark center, tipped the ball to Tyrone to start the first quarter.

Tyrone dribbled upcourt and passed to Cody. Cody bounced the ball to Anthony. He jumped up, shot, and the ball flew through the net.

"Hooray, Anthony," yelled the Shark fans.

The Jaguars had a hot streak and they made more baskets than the Sharks. They led the Sharks by eight points at half-time.

"Uh-oh," said Sarah, "the Sharks are losing."

"I bet they'll catch up," said Jennifer.

"Oh look, there's Tyrone's parents and his little brother," said Breanna, pointing to her right.

"And there's Anthony's parents and his little brother sitting in the bleachers on the other side of the gym," said Matthew.

Kayla looked around the bleachers. She saw Shannon, Grace and Julie sitting near them, in the corner.

All at once, Shannon looked up at Kayla and Jason. "Shannon keeps staring at me and Jason," said Kayla to Breanna.

"I guess she's mad jealous that you're with Jason," said Breanna.

During the third quarter, both teams kept making a lot of baskets.

"The Sharks are catching up," said Kayla to Jason.

"They just may win," laughed Jason.

Anthony dribbled upcourt. Keith, a Jaguar guard, shoved Anthony and stole the ball. Anthony slipped on the shiny wood floor.

The whistle blew. "Two foul shots for number 33," yelled the referee.

Anthony stood at the foul line. He bounced the ball twice. He looked up, shot, and it went in. Tossing the ball up high, it flew in the net again.

"Hooray Anthony," chanted the fans.

The Jaguars were leading by four points at the end of the third quarter.

"It's a close game," said Sarah.

"I'm sure we're gonna win," smiled Matthew.

When the last quarter began, Josh dribbled the ball fast upcourt. He passed to Edwin who passed to Louis. Louis shot the ball, and it went sailing through the net.

"Hooray, Sharks," yelled the fans.

Jaguars and Sharks kept scoring baskets.

"It's a tie, 64 to 64, with only two minutes to go," shouted Andrew.

"It's too close for comfort," said Breanna.

Coach Thompson called for the Shark's last time out. The team huddled together and wiped the sweat off their faces with towels.

"Hold onto the ball, stay calm and try to make more baskets," said the coach.

Josh took the ball and passed it to Tyrone. A Jaguar guard

pushed Tyrone's arm.

Shreeek! blasted the whistle. "Two foul shots for number 19," shouted the referee.

Tyrone made both foul shots. He quickly tightened the laces on his white sneakers.

"Hooray, Tyrone," yelled the fans.

Tyrone looked up at the electric scoreboard. *We're leading 66 to 64 with one minute to go*, he thought, wiping the sweat off his black curly hair.

"Hold that ball, hold that ball," chanted the Shark fans.

The Jaguar guard, Keith, took the ball, dribbling fast downcourt. He threw the ball high up in the air. The ball hit the rim and bounced in.

"Goooo Jaguars," yelled the Jaguar fans.

"It's 66 to 66," with 16 seconds to go," shouted Lakeysha to her friends.

Tyrone took the ball, dribbling fast toward the basket. *Only eight seconds to go*, he thought.

"Pass it to me," yelled Brandon, close to the basket. He passed to Brandon. Brandon jumped up, shot, and it rolled around the rim and went in.

The horn buzzed loudly.

"Yay, the Sharks won 68 to 66," screamed Marissa.

The Shark fans were cheering and stamping their feet.

Coach Thompson shook hands with the Jaguar coach.

Then the Sharks shook hands with the Jaguars. The Sharks gave each other high-fives.

Then each Shark shook hands with their coach.

"Good team work. You were great," Coach Thompson said to the players.

Jamal, Matthew and Jason gave each other high-fives up in the bleachers.

Then Matthew and Jamal slapped a double high-five to each other.

The girls hugged each other, and they all slapped high-fives.

Jason smiled at Kayla. "It was fun. See ya."

"Good-bye," said Kayla, smiling at Jason.

Sarah, Marissa, and Kayla headed for the parking lot.

Mrs. Williams was waiting in the car. They climbed into the white minivan. Breanna sat in front.

"How was the game?" asked Mrs. Williams, starting the engine and driving towards their homes.

"Terrific! The Sharks won!" Sarah exclaimed.

"I'm sure they'll make the playoffs," said Marissa.

"And let's hope the Leopards make the playoffs, too," said Mrs. Williams, driving the girls to their homes.

"Yes, and then Sarah and I will also win the bet," said Breanna.

They all laughed.

Music sounded off from the radio. Mrs. Williams drove through different housing developments as she dropped each girl off at her house.

Chapter Eighteen

PAWN SHOP

"Hi Grandma," said Kayla as she walked into the kitchen when she got home from school. Oliver jumped up and licked Kayla's hand.

"Hello," said Grandma, taking the Irish soda bread out of the oven.

"Mmm. It smells so good. You make the best Irish soda bread," said Kayla.

"When I was a little girl and I lived in Ireland, my mother used to make Irish soda bread a lot," Grandma said.

"I'm worried that Vicky and I won't get Amber's tiara back in time for our performance. We looked all over the studio," said Kayla.

Grandma wrinkled her nose. "Hmm, let me think. Oh yeah! Sometimes people sell their things to second hand stores. There's a pawn shop and even a thrift shop at the Oriole Shopping Center near your ballet school."

"Can I go now and look?" asked Kayla, jumping up and down.

Grandma sighed. "Well, I do need some groceries you can buy at the supermarket there."

"What should I buy?" asked Kayla.

"Umm, we need vegetables for dinner tonight," said her grandma. She wrote down some things she needed on a piece of paper.

"Here's two twenty dollar bills. Bring back the change," said her grandma, handing her the grocery list.

Kayla ran to her bedroom and took her savings from her bank. *Maybe I'll buy something*, she thought.

"Be back by 6:00. Bye," said Grandma.

"See ya later," Kayla said.

Kayla took her red mountain bicycle out of the garage and put her red helmet on her head. *I'll take the short cut even though there are some dirt roads*, Kayla thought.

When she got there, she parked her bike outside of the pawn shop.

Kayla walked in. She looked around and saw stamps, coins, musical instruments, jewelry and all sorts of things on the shelves.

"Hello, may I help you?" asked the salesman.

"I'm looking for a gold tiara or a crown with jewels on it," said Kayla.

The salesman raised his eyebrows. "By gosh, we do have one," he said, going into the back room.

Kayla's heart leaped. *He may have Amber's tiara*, she thought.

"Here it is," he smiled, handing her the tiara.

Kayla wrinkled her nose. "Oh no, this is all rusty. It doesn't look like it's real gold with genuine jewels."

The salesman sighed. "It's made of brass with fake jewels. I'm sorry we don't have your tiara."

"Thank you, sir," said Kayla and left.

She walked to the thrift shop, a few stores away from the pawn shop. When she went in, she saw several racks filled with second hand clothes.

"May I help you?" a saleswoman asked. She was standing behind a large counter with glass shelves.

Kayla smiled. "Do you have a gold tiara with jewels on it?"

"I don't think so, but I'll look in our storage closet," she replied.

She came back a few minutes later.

"No, I'm sorry we don't have it. Would you like something else?" the saleswoman asked.

Kayla shrugged. "Umm, I don't know."

Kayla looked at the shelves. There were all sorts of things made of china, gold and silver.

"May I see that small lady with the long dress with flowers on it?" asked Kayla.

The saleswoman put the statue on top of the counter. "It's bone china made in England," she said.

"My mother collects cups, saucers and statues made of china. I'd like to give her this lady for Christmas," said Kayla.

"We usually sell it for $99.00. But it's on sale for $45.00," said the saleswoman with a smile.

"I'll take it," Kayla said.

The woman packed it in bubble wrap and put it into a plastic bag.

"Thank you," said Kayla.

Kayla rode her bike to the back of the supermarket. She parked it in a bicycle rack. She drank water from her water bottle and munched on a green apple. Then she walked into the back of the supermarket.

I'd better hurry, thought Kayla.

She put romaine lettuce, plum tomatoes, and a cucumber in her shopping cart. She quickly found a bag of flour and a large bag of chocolate chips. Then she went to the bread aisle. She glanced up. Julien was taking a loaf of rye bread from the shelf.

"Hi Julien," said Kayla.

"Fancy meeting you here," Julien said, his blue eyes widening.

Kayla smiled. "This supermarket is a little far from my house, but I had to go to the thrift shop. I'm still looking for Amber's tiara," she blurted out.

"You shouldn't play detective. Somebody could get hurt. Anyway, Amber's tiara isn't going to make her a better dancer. My mom and I think Amy should have gotten the lead role," said Julien angrily.

"How does your father feel?" asked Kayla.

"He doesn't care whether Amy has a small or big part," said Julien.

"Somebody could get a reward for giving information

about the tiara. Wouldn't you like the reward?" asked Kayla.

Julien frowned. "I don't care about a reward. Maybe someone stole the tiara to sell it. Amy mentioned to me that Cindy told her that her father lost his job about six months ago. Cindy's mother works as a saleswoman only part-time. Cindy said they don't have enough money," he told Kayla.

"Do you think Cindy stole the tiara to sell it because she needs money?" asked Kayla.

"It could be Cindy or someone else who wants to make money. See ya," said Julien, pushing his shopping cart down the aisle.

Kayla put a loaf of whole wheat bread on her cart. She waited on line until it was her turn to pay the cashier. She put the grocery bags in her large bicycle basket, next to her china lady.

It was drizzling when she started riding home. A streak of lightning flashed ahead of her. Thunder crashed and rain came down hard. Kayla's bike kept slipping on the muddy road. But she held onto the handles tightly.

Phew, I finally got home, she thought, putting her bicycle into the garage.

Kayla went into the kitchen, handing her grandma the groceries.

"You're dripping wet. You'd better change your clothes. Your mom's coming home late so we'll have dinner soon. Please feed Oliver," Grandma said.

Kayla gave Oliver his dog food in a bowl and poured

water in his other bowl. Then she changed her clothes.

Kayla and her grandma sat at the table in the dining room.

"The pawn shop and the thrift shop didn't have the tiara," said Kayla, putting a forkful of corn in her mouth.

"That's too bad. But at least you tried," said Grandma. She placed the Irish soda bread that was on a silver plate on the table for dessert.

"Didn't you buy that silver plate in Ireland when you visited your cousins?" asked Kayla.

"Yes, and the next time I go to Ireland, you can come with me," said Grandma. She cut the soda bread into thin slices with her knife.

"I'd love to go to Ireland with you!" said Kayla, taking a bite of the soda bread. "Mmm, it's delicious!"

Chapter Nineteen

SLEIGH RIDING AND FURRY ANIMALS

Grandma and Kayla's mom picked Kayla up from school early, at 12:30 on Friday afternoon.

Kayla wore a mint green sweater, jeans, high tan suede boots and a white winter jacket. She climbed into the back seat of their blue car. Oliver, wearing a blue dog coat, jumped on her lap.

"Hi, Mom and Grandma," said Kayla.

"Hello," they said. Grandma held a container with Virginia ham that she made on her lap.

"I'm glad we're celebrating Christmas with Aunt Laura and Uncle Kevin even though it's before Christmas Day. Puleeze put the radio on one of my favorite stations," said Kayla.

They listened to music during the entire ride to New Jersey. Kayla's mom parked in front of a big white and brown split level house. She took three boxes wrapped in red and green paper out of the trunk of the car and gave them to Kayla. When they reached the house, they rang the door bell.

"Hello, Aunt Laura," Kayla said.

"Hello, Laura," said Grandma, to her youngest daughter, hugging her. When they went into the living room, Uncle

Kevin and Spencer hugged Kayla, Kayla's mom and Grandma.

A puppy started barking and jumping up on everyone.

Spencer's blue eyes narrowed. "Come here, Sandy."

Sandy went over to his master with his tail hanging down.

"This is my new puppy. He's a Golden Retriever. He's six months old," explained Spencer.

"He's precious," said Kayla, patting his head.

Spencer smiled. "He eats a lot. Come to my room. I want to show you my new computer."

Kayla, Spencer and Sandy ran up the small staircase to his bedroom.

"I like the blue painted walls and the comforter on your bed with superheroes on it. You've got a nice big screen for your computer," smiled Kayla.

"I play a lot of games on my computer," said Spencer, pushing his blond bangs out of his eyes.

"Aren't you eight years old now?" asked Kayla.

Spencer nodded. "And I'm in third grade. Do you want to take our dogs for a walk?"

"Sure!" answered Kayla.

"Mom, can Kayla and I take the dogs for a walk?" yelled Spencer, standing on the staircase.

"Alright, but don't stay out too long. Be back by 4:30."

They put on their jackets, wool hats and mittens. Then they clipped the leashes on the dogs' collars. Spencer stuffed dog biscuits, granola bars, water bottles and a compass into his jacket pockets.

"You don't need all those things. We're just taking a short walk," giggled Kayla to her cousin.

"Bye," they said, and ran out of the door.

"Let's take my sled so I can go down a hill on it. We got a lot of snow this week," said Spencer, taking his shiny wood sled out of the garage. He dragged his sled by a rope as they walked several blocks to the park.

"You wait here with the dogs. I'm going down a hill with my sled," said Spencer.

Kayla shrugged. "Okay."

Spencer climbed up the hill, carrying his sled.

"Hi, Timothy," he said to his friend when he got to the top.

"Do you want to have a race?" asked Spencer.

"Yeah," said Timothy.

The boys laid down on their stomachs on their sleds. They went sliding down the big hill.

"I won," said Spencer, jumping off his sled.

"No, I won," yelled Timothy.

Kayla walked over to them. "It looks like a tie to me," she said.

The boys slapped high-fives, and Timothy climbed back up the hill again.

"Let's slide down the hill with the doggies. My sled is big enough for all of us," said Spencer.

"Umm. I don't really want to," said Kayla.

"Just one time. Please," begged Spencer.

"Alright," said Kayla.

When they got to the top of the hill, Spencer got in front with Sandy on his lap. Kayla sat behind him with Oliver on her lap. Then she wrapped her arms around Spencer's waist. They started speeding down the hill.

Suddenly, a boy on his sled was coming towards them.

"Watch out," yelled Spencer.

The sled crashed into them, and they all fell off their sleds into the powdery snow. They could hear dogs barking in the forest near the park.

Suddenly, Sandy started running toward the forest where the dogs were barking. Spencer and Kayla, holding onto Oliver's leash, ran after Sandy into the forest. Spencer crashed into a low branch on a tree.

They stopped, panting out of breath.

"Ow, my face hurts," cried Spencer.

Kayla frowned. "You've got a few scratches on your face, and one of them is bleeding." She wiped off the blood with a tissue.

"Sandy, Sandy," shouted Kayla and Spencer together.

A gust of wind blew a huge clump of snow from the branches of a tree on top of both of their heads. They brushed the snow off their faces and clothes.

"I see furry animals!" gasped Spencer.

"Where?" asked Kayla.

"Duh! Right in front of us," said Spencer. Two brown rabbits scooted past them.

"Shh! I think I hear a dog barking," said Kayla.

Kayla held onto Oliver's leash as he started running. Oliver stopped in front of a huge tree.

"There's my doggie," said Spencer. Sandy was barking, with his black leather leash wrapped around the thick tree trunk.

"You found Sandy. Good dog," cried Kayla, hugging Oliver.

Kayla and Spencer kept on untwisting the leash until Sandy was freed from the tree.

"We'd better get out of here or else an animal may bite us," said Spencer, taking out his compass.

"Which way do you think we should go?" asked Kayla.

Spencer looked at the small round compass. "I think the forest was north of the park so let's go south," he said.

"Alright," Kayla said.

"Yikes! I see another furry animal. It's brown and white," Spencer said.

"It's a raccoon. We have to get out of here," Kayla screamed.

"Follow me," Spencer yelled, going where the needle of the compass pointed south.

They ran and ran past the snow covered trees, the dogs leading the way. Finally, they found an opening that led them out of the forest.

"Phew! You got us out of there. I'm proud of you," Kayla said, hugging him.

"Thank you," said Spencer.

He gave each dog a dog biscuit. Then Kayla and Spencer started drinking from the water bottles and munched on their granola bars.

They picked up Spencer's sled on the hill. "It's dark now," Kayla said. "They must be worried about us."

They dashed to Spencer's house.

Spencer's mom and Grandma were standing on the front porch.

"What happened to both of you? Spencer, you have scratches on your face," said his mom.

"Sandy ran into the forest, and we got lost looking for him," explained Spencer.

"You'll have to tell us the whole story later," said his mother.

Kayla and Spencer washed their hands and face. Spencer put ointment and a band-aid on his scratches.

"Dinner is ready," called Grandma.

Uncle Kevin sat at the head of the long table with an embroidered white tablecloth in the dining room. He started carving the roast turkey and the ham with his electric knife. There were bowls filled with salad, candied yams, peas and carrots, gravy and cranberry sauce on the table.

When they finished eating, Aunt Laura brought out her home-made apple pie and pecan pie with whipped cream for dessert.

"Let's give each other our gifts now," said Uncle Kevin.

He took three boxes, wrapped in red and white shiny paper, from under the Christmas tree in the living room. They all exchanged gifts and started opening them up.

"What a beautiful ballerina doll with a pink tutu and toe shoes. Thank you," smiled Kayla.

"Thanks for the sweater and games for my computer," said Spencer.

They all hugged each other and said good bye.

They scrambled into the car.

"I can't wait to go to the museum with Vicky tomorrow. We may get clues about catching the thief who stole the tiara," remarked Kayla.

"Make sure you also explore all the interesting things at the museum," said her mom.

Oliver fell asleep on Kayla's lap in the backseat during their long ride home.

Chapter Twenty

JEWEL HEIST AT THE MUSEUM

J umping up and down, Kayla and Vicky were waiting at the train station on Saturday afternoon. "I'm glad we're going to the Artifact Museum today. It's gonna be a long ride because it's way out in Suffolk County, Long Island," Kayla said.

"I can't wait to see their famous jewel collection," Vicky said.

"Thieves stole real expensive jewels from this museum. We have to find out how the robbery took place. It may give us some ideas about how Amber's tiara was stolen," Kayla said.

"We may learn something from its jewel collection and the robbery to help us find out who stole Amber's tiara," said Vicky.

When the train came, they hopped on. Vicky slid into a seat by the window, and Kayla sat beside her.

"I've got some new news to tell you. I went to a pawn shop and a thrift shop the other day to look for Amber's tiara. The thief could have sold it. But they didn't have it. Then I saw Julien in the supermarket near the thrift shop. He told me that Amy found out that Cindy's father hasn't had a job in a long time. I guess they're poor now," said Kayla.

"Cindy has two reasons to have stolen the tiara. One, she may have stolen the tiara to sell it to get money. Two, she wants her idol Amy to get the Marie part," Vicky said.

"We still need real proof before we can accuse her," said Kayla.

"Tickets please," said a woman conductor. Kayla and Vicky gave her their tickets.

"Thank you," smiled the conductor.

"Oh, I forgot to tell you. When I was leaving ballet school the other day, I hid in the bushes. I overheard Amy and Julien saying something about a tiara and in the garage. So I tried to follow them to their house. I thought they may be hiding the tiara in their garage. So I wanted to search their garage. I kept following them, but I lost them," Kayla said.

"It must have been scary," said Vicky.

"Yeah, I was really scared. It was silly of me to think I could get into their garage," Kayla said.

"It's not easy being a detective. This proves that Julien and Amy are still thinking about the tiara a lot. I guess they'd do anything for Amy to be Marie," said Vicky.

"Do you think that Julien is trying to make us believe Cindy stole the tiara to cover up that he and Amy took it?" asked Kayla.

"That's a good point. We've got to get new clues," said Vicky.

"We're finally here," Vicky said as they stepped off the train at the station. They hopped into a blue and white taxi cab to take them to the museum.

A security guard searched their pocketbooks as they entered the museum.

"This is a big museum. The jewel collection is on the fourth floor," said Kayla, reading the museum guide book.

"Let's first look at the Impressionist artists," said Vicky, walking into a large room on the first floor. They walked around looking at the paintings on the walls.

"The paintings are nice, but we have to look at the jewels," Kayla said.

"Yeah, but isn't it amazing the way the different shades of blue, green, pink, purple and orange blend together in Monet's and Renoir's paintings," said Vicky.

"C'mon. We're wasting time. We have to find out about the jewel robbery," said Kayla.

They walked into another room. "These ancient Roman and Greek vases are thousands of years old!" exclaimed Vicky.

"C'mon Vicky. Let's go," said Kayla.

They took the elevator to the fourth floor. They walked into a huge room with several glass display cases in it. There was a railing in front of them. Security guards, wearing black uniforms with gold trim, were standing in different places around the room.

"Hey, look at the sign on the display case saying, **Do Not Touch**," said Vicky, standing in front of a big jewelry collection. "The gold necklaces and bracelets are loaded with jewels and some used to belong to royalty."

Vicky and Kayla moved over to the next display. "Wow, what a big collection of tiaras!" exclaimed Kayla. "Look at that large, round crown with jewels that belonged to a king in England in the 1800's. The smaller tiaras are so delicate. They could fit on a ballerina's head."

"Oh, look at the tiara with all the diamonds and rubies on it. It once belonged to a queen of England in the 1800's," Vicky said, reading the cards about the display.

"Oh, there's a gold tiara with diamonds and pink sapphires on it. It looks like Amber's tiara," said Kayla.

Vicky nodded. "Yes, but it's larger than hers."

They moved over to another glass display case.

"Wow, that diamond on a stand is huge," said Kayla, leaning over the rail.

"I think we should talk to a guard while we're here," said Vicky. "We've got to learn more about the robbery."

Kayla nodded. "Excuse me sir," she said to a security guard, standing against a wall near them.

"Hello, young lady. Can I help you?" said a tall, muscular man, coming over to them.

Kayla cleared her throat. "I heard there was a jewel robbery in this museum a few years ago."

"Wow, you mean the big jewel heist. It was in the news, even in Europe. Some big jewels like diamonds, rubies and emeralds disappeared!" the guard exclaimed.

"How could that happen? It looks like this room has 24-hour surveillance cameras," said Vicky, pointing to the cameras hanging from the walls.

"Yes, you're right, and the display cases are made of reinforced glass with alarms in them," said the guard.

"Wow," said Kayla, leaning over the rail and touching the glass.

"On that Sunday night, no alarms or motion sensors went off and nothing showed on the camera footage," explained the guard.

"They say it could have been an inside job," said Kayla.

"Maybe it was the 24-hour security guards on duty that night, but no one knows how the robbery happened. The thieves got away with about $6 million worth of stones," said the guard. "I've got to go back on duty now."

"Thank you for talking to us," said Vicky.

"You're welcome. Have a nice day," said the guard, and he quickly stood against a wall.

They bought sandwiches, cake and soda in the museum's cafeteria and sat down at a table.

"I can't believe that the thieves could have stolen all of those jewels from such a highly guarded museum. It's shocking that they didn't even get caught. I heard that if any of those stolen jewels are sold at auctions, pawn shops or anywhere, they could trace it back to the thieves. So they can still catch those thieves," Kayla declared.

"I'm glad we came here today. The big jewel robbery in this museum makes me realize how easy it was for someone to steal Amber's tiara without getting caught," Vicky said.

"Yeah, I guess it wasn't so hard to steal Amber's tiara. The thief who stole Amber's tiara may have done it to sell it for money just like the thieves at the museum," said Kayla.

"That's true," said Vicky. "Oh, guess what? My sister Kim, who's seven years old, will be taking ballet lessons at Madame Sofia's school. A new beginner's class is starting in February. Kim will have a different teacher. Madame has a few other dance teachers at her school."

"I think your sister will have fun dancing ballet," Kayla said.

"That's true. Now let's look all over the museum at all the wonderful things it has," Vicky said.

When they finished eating their lunch, they browsed around in many of the rooms, looking at the paintings, pottery and ancient artifacts from all over the world.

"We can't look at everything. Let's go now or else we'll get home too late," said Kayla.

When they got to the station, Kayla called her mother on her cell phone to tell her what time to pick them up. "My mother will drive you home," said Kayla as they hopped on the train.

Vicky smiled. "Goody. That's nice."

Chapter Twenty-One

SKIING AND SNOW ANGELS

On Christmas Eve, Kayla looked at the boxes wrapped in shiny, colored paper under the Christmas tree in the living room. She was wearing violet cotton pajamas and tan fur-lined slippers.

Her mother and Grandma walked in.

"Can we open our presents now?" asked Kayla.

"Alright, sweetheart. This is the first time we're not getting our presents on Christmas day," answered her mom.

"It doesn't bother me because this way I can go skiing and come back in time for the Nutcracker dress rehearsal," said Kayla.

They began to open up the gift-wrapped boxes they took from under the tree.

"Thank you for the jewelry, perfume and the clothes," said Kayla, wrapping her arms around her mom and Grandma.

"Thank you Mom and Kayla for the pretty blouse and sweater," said Kayla's mother.

"I just love my new bathrobe and slippers," said Kayla's grandma.

"Mom, here's another gift from me," said Kayla, handing her a box wrapped in shiny green paper.

Kayla's mom opened it. "Oh, what a beautiful lady made in bone china. Thank you," said her mom, kissing Kayla on her cheek. She put it on the top shelf of the curio cabinet in the living room.

"I'm glad you like it," smiled Kayla.

"You'd better pack your suitcase now because we're getting up very early to make your train tomorrow," said her mom.

"Okay," Kayla said. She gave Oliver a new dog slipper. He bit into it with his teeth. Then she went to her bedroom and started putting her clothes into her suitcase.

The next morning, Kayla's mom drove Kayla to the train station in Manhattan. Kayla hugged her mom and got on the train to East Highland.

She sat near the window and read her mystery book about a boy who plays the guitar in a rock band.

When Kayla got off the train, Amanda and her father were waiting for her.

"Hi," said Kayla, hugging them.

"It's Christmas. I'm giving you money to buy a gift," said her dad.

"Oh goody. I'm going to buy an iPod," said Kayla.

They walked over to the tan SUV, and Kayla's dad put her suitcase into the trunk.

Amanda's hazel eyes lit up. "Look at my new bright blue skis on the ski-rack on top of the car. I also got new blue ski boots."

"Cool," said Kayla.

"Well, we're finally on our way to Vermont," her dad said as they drove onto the parkway.

"We're going up north but not as far as Maine," said Kayla excitedly.

They kept on driving for a few hours.

They stopped at a diner, and a waiter took their order.

"I just finished reading a mystery book on the train. It's about a boy whose expensive guitar got stolen. A boy and a girl detective search for clues until they find the thief. The thief turns out to be a boy who was a rival of the other boy," said Kayla.

"Why did he steal the guitar?" asked Amanda, taking a bite of her chicken salad sandwich.

"He stole it to stop the boy from playing in a show. Then he could play his guitar and be the star of the show. The book reminds me of Megan and Amy who are rivals of Amber. They want Amber to mess up because they want the star role," explained Kayla.

"They'd even steal her tiara," Amanda said.

"The thief could be someone you wouldn't suspect but who is very jealous of Amber," pointed out her dad.

"That could be Cindy, Nicole or Shanté. It's too bad Vicky and I only have a little more time to catch the thief at the Nutcracker dress rehearsal," said Kayla, frowning.

"Let's go now," her dad said. "It's getting late."

"Look at that sign, **Welcome to Vermont**," said Amanda

while they were riding on the parkway.

It was dark outside by the time they parked the car at the Snow Stream Hotel. Kayla opened the door to their room with their electronic card.

"Wow, what a big room with three twin beds," said Amanda.

They unpacked and put their clothes in the dresser drawers.

Kayla and Amanda called their mothers to tell them they got to the hotel.

They sat down at a table in the restaurant of the hotel.

"Aren't those two boys cute sitting at the table near the fireplace," whispered Amanda to Kayla.

"Mmm, yeah," said Kayla, putting a forkful of roast turkey in her mouth.

"Let's go to sleep early. We'll need a lot of energy to go skiing tomorrow morning," said Kayla's dad, taking a bite of blueberry pie.

The next morning, they took the hotel's shuttle bus to Mount Snow Stream Ski Resort. Kayla and her father rented skis and ski boots in the huge ski lodge.

"I signed you up for two private ski lessons. The first lesson starts in 15 minutes under the **Ski School** sign. I'm going skiing now. I'll see you later in the cafeteria for lunch," said Kayla's father.

Kayla wore her new blue ski jacket and ski pants and Amanda wore her bright pink ski jacket and ski pants.

They attached their ski boots to their skis and stood in front of a sign saying, **Ski School**.

"Hello, I'm Bridget. I'm supposed to give a private ski lesson to Kayla and Amanda."

"That's us," they said together.

"Have you ever skied before?" asked Bridget, wearing a green jacket with a badge saying ski instructor on the front.

"Yes, but only a few times," said Kayla.

"I've been skiing for a few years," said Amanda.

They pushed their skis over to the top of a beginner's slope.

"Let's first do some ski exercises. Follow me," said Bridget, tossing her blond ponytail.

Amanda and Kayla jumped up and down on their skis.

"Do you know how to do the snow plow?" asked Bridget. "It helps you slow down."

"Yes," said the girls.

"Let me see you do it," said Bridget.

The girls placed the tips of their skis together with the ends wide apart, forming a big V and snow plowed down the slope. Then they held onto the rope tow, which pulled them back up to the top of the slope.

Bridget taught them to fall facing up the slope so they wouldn't slide all the way down it. Then she showed them how to climb up a slope sideways, one ski at a time.

They practiced skiing until the lesson was over. "Good work. Now you need to practice. See ya tomorrow," said

Bridget.

After they met Kayla's dad for lunch in the cafeteria, Kayla and Amanda practiced skiing on the beginner's slope.

"Wow, you're starting to turn on your skis!" exclaimed Kayla.

"Yeah. It's fun," Amanda said.

Late in the afternoon, Kayla and her dad returned their skis and boots. Then they took the shuttle back to their hotel.

"Can we play in the snow for awhile," asked Kayla when they got back.

"Okay," said her dad, and he carried Amanda's skis back to their room.

"Let's make angels in the snow. The snow is soft and powdery," said Kayla excitedly.

They laid down in the snow on their backs and moved their arms up and down to make wings. They slowly lifted themselves up and turned around.

"Oh, what beautiful snow angels we made," said Amanda.

Kayla started leaping and spinning around in the snow. "I feel like a ballerina," said Kayla.

Amanda threw a snowball at Kayla. Kayla threw one back. They started making a lot of snowballs and threw them at each other.

After dinner, Amanda and Kayla watched cable TV in their rooms until they fell asleep.

The next morning, Bridget, Kayla and Amanda took a ski lift that had seats, with their skis sliding on the snowy ground.

They slid off and skied over to the top of the slope.

"This is just a more difficult beginner's slope. Do you know how to do the stem christie? It's the way you turn before you parallel turn." Bridget said.

"I do," said Amanda.

"I don't," said Kayla.

"I'll show you," said Bridget. She slid one ski out at a time, turning to the left and then to the right.

They practiced turning on their skis for the entire lesson.

"Your lesson is over now. Amanda, you're almost doing parallel turns. Kayla, you're turning much better now. Both of you are becoming good skiers," smiled Bridget.

"Thank you," chorused the girls.

"I enjoyed teaching you girls. Have fun on the slopes. Good-bye," said Bridget, and she zig-zagged down the slope.

Kayla and Amanda went into the ski lodge to have lunch in the cafeteria.

Chapter Twenty-Two

DARE AND DOUBLE DARE

After lunch, Amanda and Kayla waited on a ski lift line of the more difficult beginner slope later on in the afternoon.

"Hi," said a boy with blue eyes and blond hair, standing behind them. "I'm Luke and this is my friend Ryan. We've seen you in the restaurant at the hotel we're staying at," he said.

"We've also seen you guys there," said Amanda.

"Brrr, it's freezing even with the sun shining," said Ryan, pulling down his blue wool hat over his wavy brown hair. "The lift lines for the beginners' slopes are so long, and they are too short."

"We're only taking this slope one time to really speed down it," said Luke.

"The intermediate slopes have a lot of long trails and are more fun. Come ski with us," said Ryan.

"I'm sort of a beginner," said Kayla.

"Can you turn when you're skiing?" asked Luke.

"Sure," said Kayla.

"I'm starting to parallel turn," said Amanda.

"The intermediate slopes are only a little harder. C'mon," urged Ryan.

Kayla shook her head no. "I think I'll stay on the beginner slopes."

"I dare you to go," said Luke.

"Umm, I don't think so," said Kayla.

"I double dare you," said Ryan with a grin.

Kayla rolled her eyes. "Oh, alright."

"Do you promise to ski with us the entire time?" asked Amanda.

Luke smiled. "Yeah, let's go."

They pushed their skis, using their ski poles, to another ski lift.

"How old are you guys?" asked Kayla as they waited on the line.

"I'm 13 and Luke is 12," answered Ryan.

"It's our turn," said Luke. The boys quickly got on the seat for two as their skis slid along the snow covered ground. "See you at the top," he said.

The girls got on the lift in back of the boys.

"Uh-oh, this lift is going up very high. Look at how small the trees and houses look below us," gasped Kayla.

"The people look so little," said Amanda, looking down.

As they jumped off the lift, Kayla fell down. Amanda helped her up.

The boys were waiting for them at the top of the slope. The girls skied over to them.

"Eww, it's too steep. I think it's an advanced slope," said Kayla, looking down the slope.

"It's really an intermediate slope," said Ryan.

"But you'll be okay. The first slope is the steepest. The rest of the slopes and trails are easier," said Luke.

Oh, no, I've only skied on beginner slopes, thought Kayla.

"Do the snow plow," called Amanda as she and the boys started skiing down the slope.

"C'mon Kayla, we're waiting for you," yelled Amanda, at the bottom of the slope.

"Yo hurry up," yelled Ryan. "I'm freezing."

Kayla was thinking, *I'm terrified, but I'd better go down. What if I get frostbite on my fingers and toes. I can't make them wait. I don't even see them.*

Kayla started doing the snow plow down the slope, her heart beating fast.

Oh no, the slope is very icy, thought Kayla. As she skied over a patch of ice, one of her skis went up in the air.

All of a sudden, a boy started skiing toward her. He slipped on a huge patch of ice and crashed into her. He grabbed onto her shoulder, and they both started speeding down the slope. They fell and went sliding down the slope until they reached the bottom.

"Are you alright?" Amanda cried.

"Ow," cried Kayla, trying to get up. "My ankle hurts. I can't stand on it," she said, sitting in the snow. Her skis fell off.

"I'm sorry I crashed into you. I slipped on the ice. Can I help you?" the boy asked.

Kayla frowned. "No, but it's okay."

145

"Bye," he said, and he skied down the trail.

Just then, a gray-haired man skied over to them with a ski patrol badge on his green jacket.

"Hi, I'm Artie. Can I help you?" he asked.

"I hurt my ankle, so I can't ski anymore," said Kayla.

"Don't worry. I'll take you down by sled," said Artie. He called the ski patrol office on his cell phone.

They waited until a man came with the sled.

"Hi Eugene," said Artie.

They tied rope from the sled to the back of Artie's buckle on his jacket.

Eugene took Kayla's skis and went skiing down the slope.

Kayla laid down in the sled, and Artie covered her with a blanket. He tied rope around Kayla so she couldn't fall out.

"We'll see you back at the ski lodge," said Amanda. Ryan, Luke and Amanda waved good-bye and started skiing down the trail.

Artie started skiing down the trails with the rope pulling Kayla in the sled behind him.

My stomach feels like jelly. Wow, what a bumpy ride. There's so many long hills and narrow trails. I'm scared we're gonna crash, thought Kayla.

When they reached the bottom of the entire slope, Artie helped her walk to the First Aide station, next to the ski lodge.

"Thank you," said Kayla, shaking his hand.

"Bye," said Artie with a grin.

"You sprained your ankle just a little bit. Try to stay off it as much as possible for a day or two. Use this ice pack a few times today," said the nurse.

Oh dear, I hope my ankle doesn't bother me when I dance at the performance. I practiced so hard for months, and the other girls depend upon me, thought Kayla.

She limped into the lodge, holding an ice pack. "How are you?" asked Kayla's father, rushing over to her.

"I'm okay," Kayla said.

They took the shuttle bus back to the hotel.

The next morning they ate breakfast in the restaurant.

"It's our last day here. And tonight we're going to the disco party in our hotel for girls and boys 11 and up," said Amanda.

"How does your ankle feel?" asked Kayla's dad.

"It hurts a little when I walk on it, but it feels much better," said Kayla.

"That's good," said her dad.

"By the way, how's your guinea pig doing?" Kayla asked, swirling maple syrup around her French toast.

"Daisy's cute, and she's getting much bigger," Amanda said.

"I still don't know whether I want to take toe dancing lessons," admitted Kayla.

"You'll be a real ballerina when you're dancing on your toes," Amanda said.

"Follow your dreams, no matter what," said her dad.

"I guess I can't ski today," said Kayla.

"No, of course not! Just stay in the ski lodge and relax," said her dad.

"Alright," Kayla said.

When they got to the lodge, Kayla sat on a chair near the fireplace and watched the people coming in and out of the lodge. Then she read her magazine.

"Hi," said Amanda, coming into the lodge, later on. "Let's eat lunch." After Kayla and Amanda ate lunch, Amanda went skiing again.

Maybe I'll buy something nice in the ski store, Kayla thought. She walked into the ski store in the lodge. She looked at sweaters, ski pants, jackets, hats and mittens. She passed the children's toys and games.

Then she stopped at the counter where they sold souvenirs. She looked at the Vermont maple syrup, sugar cane and candy. She picked up a small green pillow with a picture of trees on top of it. *Mmm, it smells like pine trees. I may buy it,* she thought.

Then Kayla stopped at a counter that had purses made of silk and leather wallets and belts.

Then a girl, wearing a yellow sweater, came over and started looking at the purses. She picked up a small, black silk purse.

Then Kayla walked over to the next counter that was filled with costume jewelry. She picked up a gold earring with a star hanging on it. A woman and her two daughters came over and started looking at the necklaces.

Just then, the girl with the yellow sweater came over to the jewelry counter and looked at the bracelets. She tried a silver bracelet on her wrist. She put it down and started walking toward the exit.

"Stop, stop," yelled a saleswoman, running over to the girl with the yellow sweater. But the girl started walking out the exit. The saleswoman grabbed onto her sweater.

"Let go of me!" yelled the girl.

"I saw you take a black silk purse," said the saleswoman.

"No, I didn't," said the girl, tossing her brown ponytail.

The saleswoman looked flustered. "I think you're hiding it under your sweater. Please pick up your sweater," she demanded.

"Leave me alone. I didn't take anything," said the girl.

Kayla watched them. Then a lot of people started staring at them.

"If you don't lift up your sweater, I'll call the police," the saleswoman said with a frown.

The girl picked up her sweater and a small, black, silk purse fell on the floor. "I took it by accident," she said, tears running down her cheeks.

The saleswoman picked up the purse. "How old are you?" she asked.

"I'm 13," replied the girl, her head bent down.

"You should never steal anything again or you'll get into a lot of trouble. I'm not going to report this to the police," the saleswoman said.

The girl nodded. "Thank you," she said, running out of the store.

I feel so sorry for the girl. I hope she doesn't steal anymore, thought Kayla.

"May I help you?" asked a salesman.

"Yes," said Kayla. She paid for the maple syrup, pillow and candy made in Vermont.

The salesman put them in a plastic bag and handed it to her. "Enjoy them," he said.

Later on in the afternoon, Amanda came into the lodge and sat next to Kayla near the fireplace.

"Hi," said Amanda. "I'm not skiing anymore today, but your dad's still skiing with his friend Barry."

Kayla told Amanda about what happened in the ski store. "The girl stole the purse because she didn't have the money to pay for it. Whoever stole the tiara may have done it to sell it just for the money," explained Kayla.

"I agree with you. The person who stole the tiara could be a girl like this girl who stole the purse," said Amanda.

Kayla nodded her head. "Oh, I just thought of something else. Whoever stole the tiara may be sorry and want to return it. But the person is afraid they'll call the police and press charges," said Kayla.

"Yeah," Amanda agreed.

Kayla, Kayla's dad and Amanda took the shuttle back to the hotel.

After dinner, Kayla and Amanda changed into their party

clothes. Kayla wore a pink silk blouse, a black velvet miniskirt and black patent leather low-heeled shoes. Amanda wore a silver mini dress and silver low heels. They both put on their pink lip gloss.

"It's pretty dark in here," said Amanda as they walked into the disco room that night.

"The blinking colored lights and the big silver ball hanging above the dance floor are awesome," said Kayla.

They stood at a long table filled with refreshments. Chips, dips, cookies, cake and soda were on it.

"Yo hiya," Ryan called as he and Luke walked over to the girls.

"Hey, Kayla, how's your ankle?" asked Luke.

"It's much better," smiled Kayla.

"Do you want to dance?" Ryan asked Kayla.

"Okay," smiled Kayla.

"Would you like to dance?" Luke asked Amanda.

"Okay," Amanda said.

Then Kayla and Ryan started dancing on the dance floor. Amanda and Luke danced near them.

"Let's go to the game room," Ryan said.

When they got to the game room, they started playing all kinds of groovy games together.

"We have to go now. We have to get up real early tomorrow to drive back to East Highland," said Amanda.

"We also have to leave early to get back to Connecticut," said Luke.

"It was nice meeting you guys," said Kayla.

"We hope we get to see you girls again and go skiing together," said Ryan.

"Kayla, I bet you become a great skier," said Luke.

They all burst out laughing.

"Good-bye," said the girls and headed back to their room.

The next morning at 5:00, on Saturday, Amanda, Kayla and her father ate breakfast and then started driving back to East Highland. When they got there, they first stopped at Amanda's house.

"Hello," said Aunt Carolyn, coming out of the house. "Did you have a good time?"

"Yes," they all agreed.

"Thank you Uncle Dan," said Amanda, hugging him.

"I'll be back during my February winter vacation," said Kayla.

They all hugged and said good-bye.

"We've got to hurry and make the 12:00 train. This is some tight squeeze to get you back in time for your dress rehearsal," said her dad, driving to the station.

"I hope we find good clues at the dress rehearsal," remarked Kayla.

"Vicky and you are good detectives even if you don't crack the case," said her dad. "I'll be driving to Long Island tomorrow to see the performance."

When they got there, Kayla kissed her dad on his cheek and wheeled her suitcase on the train. She sat down next to a lady with a black toy poodle on her lap and a parakeet in a cage on the floor.

Kayla took out her notebook and started reading the clues and suspects written in it. *Julien, Cindy, Amy and Megan have the most clues leading to them. Maybe we can trick the thief to get to the truth*, she thought.

Kayla walked over to her mother when she got off the train. "How was skiing?" asked her mom, driving back to Long Island.

"I'm just a beginner, but I had a great time. I sprained my ankle a little, but it feels much better now," Kayla said.

"I'm glad it's alright," her mom said, relieved.

"Yeah," Kayla said.

"We made it just in time for your dress rehearsal," said her mom, driving into the parking lot of the ballet theater. "Bye, honey bun."

"Bye," Kayla said, climbing out of the car.

Chapter Twenty-Three

A GLITTERY SURPRISE AT DRESS REHEARSAL

She hurried into the girls' dressing room of the theatre at 4:45 in the afternoon. Kayla changed into a black leotard and put on her pink leather ballet shoes. Then she went into the small dance studio.

"Hi," Kayla said, going over to Vicky at the barre.

"Hello," said Vicky. "Everyone finished doing their exercises and left to change into their costumes."

"I just got back from my ski trip. I'm glad I'm only a little late," said Kayla.

After they did their warm-up exercises, they went into the costume room. They took their long pink tutus off the hangers.

Amy came in and took her white dress with a short tutu off the hanger. "Oh no, my dress is ripped," she yelled.

Madame walked into the room. "Someone tore my dress," cried Amy.

"Maybe you caught it on something," said Madame.

Amy shook her head. "I think one of the dancers did it to stop me from being the Sugar Plum Fairy."

"That's nonsense. At the end of the dress rehearsal, give your dress to Joan Etta, the costume designer. She'll have it sewn before the show tomorrow night," Madame said.

Amy frowned. "Alright."

"Girls, hurry up and change into your costumes," said Madame to Amy, Kayla and Vicky.

Kayla and Vicky went into separate dressing booths lined up against a wall and changed into their costumes. They went back to their lockers and put their clothes in them.

"Oh, there's Amy putting on her make-up," Kayla said.

Then Amy left the dressing room.

"Oh look at all the pink glitter on the floor. It must have come off our dresses," said Vicky.

"I have new ballet shoes with ribbons for my flower costume. But I don't know how to tie them," sighed Kayla.

"I'll help you tie them," said Vicky.

"Gee, thanks," smiled Kayla.

Vicky helped Kayla tie the pink ribbons around her ankles.

Then they started putting on their make-up at the dressing table. Suddenly, they heard someone screaming.

"It sounds like it's coming from the stage," Vicky said as they ran there.

They found Amber sitting on the floor backstage, wearing her long pink dress. Many dancers were crowded around her.

"What happened to you?" asked Madame.

"Someone pushed me very hard, and I fell. I bruised my elbow, and it's a little red," moaned Amber.

"It may have been an accident," said Madame, putting her hand on her forehead.

"No way. It was on purpose," sobbed Amber.

"Will you be able to dance?" asked Madame.

"Yes, it only hurts a little bit," said Amber.

"I'm glad you're okay. I want everyone to finish putting on their make-up and costumes now," Madame called out, and she hurried away.

"Amber, where were you when you got pushed and fell on the floor?" asked Kayla.

"I think I was walking past the giant candy canes and ice cream cones. I'm a little confused," Amber said nervously.

"Did you notice anyone near you?" asked Vicky.

"Umm, I saw a few girls I didn't know. Umm, oh yeah, I also saw Shanté taking photos with her cell phone. But nobody was very close to me. Whoever pushed me must have run away quickly," explained Amber.

"Could you tell whether it was a girl or a boy?" asked Vicky.

Amber shook her head. "No way! But I've got to go now and put my make-up on. I'm in Scene 1," she said, walking away.

"Let's look for clues," said Vicky. "We need all the help we can get."

They started looking all over the floor, backstage.

Kayla squatted down on her knees. "Oh, look! There's white glitter under the candy canes," she gasped.

Then Vicky squatted down on her knees and looked under the vanilla and strawberry ice cream cones. "I see a little white glitter here too," said Vicky.

"Who has white glitter on their costumes?" asked Kayla.

"The snow fairies," said Vicky.

"Amy and Megan also have white glitter on their costumes," said Kayla.

"Let's save the glitter. It could be an important clue," said Vicky.

Kayla and Vicky bent down on their knees and picked up the white glitter. They held it in their hands and headed to the dressing room. They put the glitter in a ziplock plastic bag.

"I also have the other three ziplock bags," Kayla said, taking them out of her ballet bag. "One has the gold barrette, another has the diamond and the other one has the pink sapphire chip."

"I see some pink glitter mixed in the white glitter," said Vicky, looking through her magnifying glass.

Kayla looked through the magnifying glass. "Wow, you're right!"

"The flower costumes and Amy's costume has pink glitter on them," said Vicky.

"Whoever pushed Amber may have pink or white glitter on their costumes," said Kayla.

"We better put on our make-up now," said Vicky.

They got their own make-up bags and sat down at the dressing tables. Looking into the mirror, they first put powder on their faces. Then they put on eyebrow pencil, blue eye shadow, eye liner, mascara, rouge and red lipstick.

"Oh, I just realized that Shanté must have taken photos on the camera on her cell phone. Let's ask Shanté if we can look at her photos," Kayla said.

"We may find a clue in them," added Vicky.

They went backstage but couldn't find Shanté.

They went over to the stage. Madame was standing there.

"Have you seen Shanté?" asked Kayla.

"She just left because she wasn't feeling well. She'll be back tomorrow for the performance," said Madame.

"Oh well, I guess we'll have to wait until tomorrow to see the photos before the performance starts," Vicky said softly to Kayla.

"This is terrible news. We really need to see the photos now," whispered Kayla.

"But we can't see them now. Let's look backstage again for more clues," said Vicky.

Kayla squattered under the cardboard lollypops. "I don't see anything."

Vicky and Kayla walked all around backstage. They saw a door. "This could be a storage room. We may find some clues in it," said Vicky. She jiggled the door knob, but the door was locked.

They looked under all the trees and under the ice cream cones.

"There's something white under the vanilla ice cream cone," said Kayla, picking it up. "It's a round, white barrette," she gasped. "I didn't see it there before now."

"Who do you think it belongs to?" asked Vicky.

"Amy and I bought the same white barrettes at the mall. It could be Amy's or another girl's barrette," Kayla told Vicky.

"It's a good clue, but it doesn't prove that Amy pushed Amber," Vicky replied.

Kayla took out her ballet bag when they reached her locker. "I'll put the white barrette in the same bag as the gold barrette," Kayla declared. "Oh, no, I got some dirt on my costume." She washed some of the dirt off with water from the sink.

"Everybody come in the theater now," Madame shouted.

"Hurry or we'll be late," said Vicky. They finished putting on their make-up and dashed over to the stage.

"Attention everyone," said Madame, standing on the stage. "We're starting our rehearsal now. You may stay in the dressing rooms now, until Jerry, the stage manager, calls on you. Then you'll wait in the wings until it's your turn to perform. But just for the dress rehearsal, you may prefer to sit in the audience until Jerry calls you."

"Let's stay in the theatre and watch the rehearsal," Kayla said. They sat in the first row.

"All the dancers in Act 1, Scene 1, come on the stage now," called out Madame.

Amber wore her long pink dress and her long, red hair was in a pony tail. The other girls and boys wore their party clothes. They danced in front of the Christmas tree in the large living room.

During Scene 2, the toy soldiers were dressed in their red jackets and white pants. They started fighting with the huge gray mice with their swords in the living room. Amber started dancing in the wrong direction and tripped on her long, white nightgown. She crashed into a toy soldier. They both fell down. A stagehand turned off the CD on the stereo.

"Amber, if you cannot pay attention, Amy or Megan may have to take your place as Marie," said Madame.

"I I I'm sorry," stammered Amber, tears running down her cheeks.

"It's alright. Now focus on being Marie," said Madame with a smile. Then Madame sat in the first row to watch everyone dance.

"If we don't find out who's behind all of this soon, Amber may fall apart," said Vicky to Kayla.

Katie, a stagehand, turned on the music on the stereo again.

When the mice disappeared, Dylan, the Nutcracker, dressed like a toy soldier, put the King of Mice's plastic gold crown on Amber's head. Then he turned into a handsome prince.

"Everyone take a 20 minute break, while the stagehands change the scenery to the snow forest," called out Madame.

Megan yelled out, "Someone stole my make-up bag," as Kayla and Vicky went into the dressing room.

"Megan, maybe you misplaced your make-up," said Madame, overhearing her yelling. "You may use the make-up that's on the dressing table."

"Alright," said Megan, and she stomped off.

Just then, Cindy screamed, "My gold bracelet is missing!"

"Oh dear, perhaps it just fell off your wrist because the clasp was loose," Madame said.

"I'll look for it now," said Cindy.

"No, look for it later. We must start rehearsing now," said Madame.

At that moment, the janitor started sweeping the floor.

"Excuse me," said Vicky, almost tripping over the broom.

"Watch your step or you'll fall," smiled the janitor, winking his eye at her.

"Oh, okay," Vicky replied. "Hey, I have an idea. Let's look in the orchestra pit for clues," she said.

Kayla and Vicky climbed down the little stairs to the orchestra.

"There's only a piano here now. Madame said that in some of the ballets she uses a small orchestra with the piano, violins and a few other instruments," said Kayla.

"She feels that a big stereo system is better for the Nutcracker. Anyway, it's possible that someone hid the tiara in here," said Vicky.

They looked all over the cement floor. "Oh, here's a silver hair clip," said Kayla, picking it up. "Many girls use these. It's not a good clue," she said, tossing it on the floor.

Vicky turned the knob of a door, and it opened. They

walked into a tiny room. "It's dark in here," she said, turning on the light.

"I'll close the door so no one will find us in here. This must be a storage room," said Kayla.

"There's a lot of musical instruments stuffed together on the shelves. Eww, this violin and the drums are full of dust," said Vicky, touching them.

"Look at all the jewelry and the other small props on the shelves," said Kayla.

"These wigs are cool," said Vicky, trying on a wig with long red hair. Kayla tried on a wig with two long blond braids.

Suddenly, the door started opening. "Hide," Kayla said. They hid behind a large shelf with drums on it.

They heard someone come inside the room and close the door. Then they heard footsteps.

"I wish whoever it is would leave," whispered Kayla, her heart racing.

"Kayla and Vicky, stop hiding. I know you're in here," called out a boy.

Vicky and Kayla slowly came out from hiding. "Dylan, what are you doing here?" Vicky asked.

"I saw you sneak in here, so I decided to follow you. What are you doing in here?" Dylan asked.

"To tell you the truth, we're looking for Amber's tiara," admitted Vicky.

"Do you have any idea who stole the tiara?" Kayla asked.

"Umm, let me think. Maybe a ghost did it," Dylan

remarked.

Kayla frowned. "Stop kidding around."

"Maybe someone stole it to sell it," Dylan said.

"Or someone stole it to stop Amber from being Marie," Vicky added.

"Let's look around in here a little more," Kayla said. They started walking around the small room.

"Hey, I found a tiara, but it's made of metal," Dylan said, putting it on his head.

Just then they heard Madame yelling.

"Our break is over. Madame wants us to come now," Vicky said.

"We'd better go. But if I get any news about the tiara, I'll let you know," Dylan said.

Dylan, Kayla and Vicky raced up the stairs. Dylan ran backstage. Kayla and Vicky sat in the first row of the theatre and watched the ice fairies twirl around in the fake snow.

Then the stagehands changed the scenery to the palace in the Land of Sweets. They put the candy canes, lollypops and ice cream cones painted on thick cardboard stands along the sides of the stage.

"Act 2 will begin now," called out Madame.

Marie and the prince sat on a golden throne in the palace. The first dance started. Megan wore a brown shirt and a long white tutu with white glitter on it. Connor wore a brown shirt and white pants. They danced together in the Dance of Hot Chocolate.

"Megan and Connor danced very well together," said Vicky to Kayla.

A girl danced in the Dance of Coffee. Then a girl and a boy jumped out of a giant teapot wearing blue silk costumes, to perform the Dance of China. Then the three candy canes came onstage and leaped through hoops.

Mother Ginger danced onto the stage next. Seven children came out from under her huge hoopskirt and did a little dance.

"The Waltz of Flowers is next," yelled Jerry.

Kayla and Vicky waited in the left wing with the other girls wearing flower costumes.

Then, the eight girls, wearing long tutus in different shades of pink and red, twirled around the stage. Kayla spun around too fast and bumped into Shanté who bumped into Nicole. All three fell down and slowly got up.

"You dance like a hippo," said Nicole to Kayla.

"I'm sorry," said Kayla. *I'm so embarrassed*, she thought.

The Sugar Plum Fairy danced with the prince. Dylan tripped as he tried to lift up Amy, and they fell on the floor.

"Try it again," Madame said.

Dylan lifted up Amy with both hands and gently put her down.

"Amy has white barrettes in her hair. The one we found could be hers," whispered Kayla to Vicky," standing on the stage with the other dancers in the Land of Sweets.

When Marie and the prince started to fly away in a sleigh, raised above the stage by wires, it started swaying back and forth and tipped over. Amber and Dylan quickly jumped off the sleigh.

"Attention everybody," called out Madame. "Please hang up your costumes in the costume room. Be back here at 6:00 tomorrow night. The performance starts at 8:00."

Kayla and Vicky changed into their clothes. "Let's get here very early so we can look for more clues," whispered Kayla to Vicky.

"It's our last chance to get the tiara back so Amber can wear it at the performance," Vicky said.

"Amy, Julien, Megan and Cindy are the suspects with the strongest motives to have stolen the tiara. But we need solid evidence to catch the thief," said Kayla.

"The janitor could also be a suspect," said Vicky.

"But he doesn't want to be Marie or the Sugar Plum Fairy," laughed Kayla.

"He seemed nice when he smiled at me today. I'll see you tomorrow night," Vicky said, dashing out of the theater.

Kayla rushed to the parking lot. Her mother was waiting for her in their dark blue car.

"So how was the dress rehearsal?" asked her mom.

"Good, but we have so little time left to find the thief," Kayla said.

Her mother frowned. "Many mysteries do not get solved. Please forget about being a detective and concentrate on your dancing."

"Yeah, okay. I'm really excited about our performance

tomorrow night," said Kayla.

"I can't wait to see it," smiled her mom. "Your dad, Grandma and I will be cheering for all of you."

"Thats' nice," giggled Kayla.

Chapter Twenty-Four

A BOX OF TUTUS

Sunday, the next night, Kayla got to the theater at 6:00. She changed into her leotard and ballet shoes. Then she and Vicky did warm-up exercises in the small dance studio.

"Let's look for Shanté. We've got to see those photos," said Vicky.

They looked in the dressing room, but Shanté wasn't there.

They walked into the theater which was empty.

"Oh there's Shanté standing on the stage. She's taking a photo of the Christmas tree with her silver cell phone," said Kayla. They climbed up on the stage.

"Hi, Shanté. Why are you taking photos of the scenery?" asked Vicky.

"My grandmother is sick. She can't come to the ballet tonight. I'm taking photos of some of the dancers and scenery to show her when I visit her in Baltimore, Maryland," explained Shanté.

"Can we please look at all the photos you took yesterday? It may help us find out who pushed Amber," said Kayla.

"Oh no, my photos have nothing to do with that," said

Shanté with a frown.

"We need to look at those photos," said Kayla.

"No, you can't see them," said Shanté, holding her cell phone up in the air.

As Vicky tried to grab the cell phone, Shanté dropped it on the floor. Vicky snatched it. Then she and Kayla raced into a storage room and slammed the door. Then Vicky quickly locked it.

"Let me in," yelled Shanté, banging on the door. "Give me back my cell phone."

"Just ignore her," said Vicky.

Vicky held the cell phone and pressed menu. Then she clicked onto photos. Then they started searching the photos for clues.

"Vicky, slow down, you're going too fast," Kayla said.

"Hey, look at the photo of the lollypops. Now look at the gum drops," Vicky said. "These are the photos that were taken yesterday."

"Here's the strawberry, vanilla and chocolate ice cream cones. Next are the candy canes. Stop! I can't believe it! Look at the candy canes," Kayla cried.

"There's Megan standing behind Amber in front of the candy canes!" gasped Vicky.

Vicky opened the door. Shanté was waiting outside the door. "I want my phone back now," Shanté said angrily.

"Shanté, by accident, you took a photo of Megan pushing Amber when you took a photo of the candy canes. We have to borrow your cell phone to show it to Madame," said Kayla.

"We'll return it to you later," said Vicky.

"I don't believe you. Give me back my phone," yelled Shanté.

"Here, look at this photo!" said Vicky, holding onto the small phone.

"Oh no, it looks like Megan did it," gasped Shanté. "Megan's my friend, but you've got to show it to Madame," she sighed. Then she headed toward the dressing room.

"We've got to find Megan now," said Vicky to Kayla.

They ran backstage, but they didn't find her. They raced to the small dance studio, but she wasn't there. Then they went into the girls' dressing room. They walked up and down the aisles.

"Oh there's Megan, sitting on the bench," said Kayla. They rushed over to her. Megan was tying the ribbons around her white ballet shoes.

"What do you want?" asked Megan, looking up at them.

"Did you push Amber backstage yesterday?" asked Kayla.

Megan glared at them. "No, of course not! How dare you accuse me."

"We have proof," said Vicky. She held onto the cell phone tightly and showed Megan the photo.

Megan's brown eyes widened. "I I I'm just standing next to her," she stammered.

"If you look very closely, your hand is touching Amber's

back," said Vicky.

Kayla glared at Megan. "You pushed Amber and stole her tiara, so you would get to be Marie. Even though you and Amy are the understudies for Marie, you were sure Madame would choose you. That's because you think you're the best dancer."

"Even if Madame chose Amy to replace Amber as Marie, you knew you'd be the Sugar Plum Fairy," said Vicky.

"If you got rid of Amber, you'd win either way," said Kayla.

Vicky's eyes were blazing. "You may have even torn Amy's dress hoping to upset the other understudy to make sure you'd be Marie."

"I didn't tear Amy's dress," snapped Megan.

"But you stole Amber's tiara hoping she'd be too upset to be a great ballerina," said Kayla, her heart pounding.

"No, I didn't," yelled Megan.

"Yes, you did push Amber and steal her tiara. Y Y You can't deny it anymore," stammered Vicky.

"The photo tells it all," said Kayla.

"Oh, alright. I I did it. I pushed her, but I never wanted to hurt her," stammered Megan.

"Admit it! You pushed Amber to stop her from dancing, and you stole her tiara!" said Kayla, tears running down her face.

"Yes. I'm very sorry. I wanted to be the star. I realize now that I'll never be a great ballerina by hurting someone else. That's cheating," sobbed Megan, tears running down her cheeks.

Kayla took a deep breath. "Maybe there's something else that's really bothering you," she said.

"Well, I'm always babysitting for my baby brother because my parents work a lot. I don't have friends anymore, because I don't have any time to go out with them," confessed Megan, her head bent down.

Vicky sighed, "That's not fair."

"Hey, did you find your make-up bag?" asked Kayla.

"Yeah, I left it at my house. I really wish I could do something to help," said Megan, her shoulders slumped down.

"You can. Tell us where you put the tiara," said Vicky.

"I really wanted to return it. I had hidden it in my bedroom closet. Then I brought the tiara back and put it in a storage room," admitted Megan.

"Where is the storage room?" asked Vicky.

"In this theater," said Megan.

"I thought most of the storage rooms were all locked," said Kayla.

"Not the one where I hid the tiara in," said Megan.

They raced backstage and Megan led them into a storage room. There were a lot of props on the shelves. There were many boxes all over the floor.

"I put it in a box filled with tutus, but I I forgot which box it is," said Megan, her voice trembling.

"We have to look in the boxes," said Vicky.

They started opening up all the boxes.

"Oh, I found the tutus," said Kayla. She tossed out yellow, pink and white short tutus until the box was empty. "There's no tiara in this box."

"Keep looking," shouted Vicky. "There are probably more boxes filled with tutus."

They opened several more boxes filled with different kinds of props, ballet clothes and tutus.

"I think I found it," yelled Vicky, tossing out pink tutus from a box until it was empty.

"Oh, now I remember. There were different colored tutus in the box. They were all long tutus," said Megan, putting her hand on her forehead.

They kept on looking in other boxes.

"Maybe someone found the tiara already," said Megan.

"But no one else knows where you hid it. Let's keep looking," urged Kayla.

They started opening more boxes. Megan started tossing out blue, yellow and pink tutus from a box.

Vicky watched Megan. "Hey, those tutus are all long."

"I found it," screamed Megan, picking up the tiara from the bottom of the box.

"I can't believe we found it," gasped Vicky. "Give me the tiara." Megan handed it to Vicky. Vicky held it tightly.

"This is wonderful. We've got to give it to Amber right away," said Kayla, jumping up and down.

They looked all over the theatre.

Finally, they found Amber backstage.

"We found your tiara," said Megan, panting out of breath.

"Here it is," Vicky said, giving it to Amber.

"Where did you find it?" Amber asked.

Vicky showed her the photo on the cell phone. Then she told her how they got Megan to admit everything she did.

"So it was you all along, stealing my tiara, pushing me, trying to stop me from being Marie," said Amber angrily, tears running down her face.

Just then, Madame came backstage. "Vicky and Kayla, why aren't you in your costumes yet?" she asked.

"I got my tiara back," said Amber, holding it close to her.

Madame's mouth opened up wide. "Where did you find it?" she cried.

Vicky showed the photo to Madame and told her everything that had happened.

"I'm shocked," gasped Madame.

"I I I'm sorry. I was wrong. I'll never hurt anyone again," stammered Megan.

"You should only dance your best and enjoy yourself. You can only hope you'll get a star role someday. I'll only allow you to continue taking ballet lessons at my school on one condition. You have to see a therapist or a counselor. You need someone you can trust to talk to and help you solve your problems," said Madame, with tears in her eyes.

"I promise I'll go to a therapist," declared Megan, tears rolling down her face.

"What should we tell everyone?" Kayla asked.

"Let's stick to the truth. We'll tell everyone that Vicky and Kayla found out that Megan took the tiara. We'll also tell them that Megan is very sorry, and she promised that she'll never do that again," Madame explained.

"That's a good idea," Vicky agreed.

"I must tell Shanté that I have to keep her cell phone until I show the photo to Megan's parents," Madame said.

"Shanté's photo gave us the proof we needed," Vicky said.

Madame nodded. "Now hurry up and finish putting on your costumes and make-up. The show starts in 20 minutes. Oh dear, I've got a headache," she mumbled, putting her hand on her head. Then she walked away.

Amber smiled. "Both of you are the greatest detectives. Thank you very much," she said.

"I'm so relieved that we found it," Vicky said. Kayla and Vicky hugged Amber.

"Let's get ready," Amber said. They dashed to the dressing room.

Kayla and Vicky stood in the left wing peeking out from the blue velvet curtains. The house lights were still on.

"Wow, what a big crowd. There won't be any empty seats. Oh look, my parents, Kim, and my aunt and uncle are sitting in the first row," said Vicky, hopping up and down.

"Oh, my father made it here in time. He's sitting next to my mom and Grandma in the third row," said Kayla, spinning around.

"We'd better wait in the dressing room," said Vicky, and they scampered away.

The house lights dimmed, and the music went on. The curtains went up, and the stage lights shined brightly.

The dancers in the dressing rooms could hear the music coming from the loud speakers in the wall. That way they knew what was happening on the stage.

Vicky and Kayla sneaked to the left wing again, just in time to see the Nutcracker place the King of Mice's crown on Marie's head. Then he magically turned into a handsome prince.

"I'm so happy Amber is wearing her own gold tiara with the sparkling jewels for the crown," whispered Vicky.

Kayla nodded. "It fits perfectly on her head."

Then they tiptoed back to the dressing room.

Jerry, the stage manager, came into the dressing room and told the three candy canes, Mother Ginger and her seven children to wait in the right wing.

A few minutes later, Jerry came back into the dressing room.

"You're next," he told the eight girls in flower costumes. They tiptoed to the left wing of the stage and waited.

"I feel nervous," whispered Vicky to Kayla.

"I feel like I have butterflies in my stomach," said Kayla.

"Cindy, what happened to your bracelet?" Vicky asked.

"Oh, I found my bracelet under my locker this evening. I guess I didn't put the clasp on right," admitted Cindy. She showed her gold bracelet on her wrist to Kayla and Vicky.

When Mother Ginger and her children's dance was over, Jerry told the flowers it was their turn.

Kayla, Vicky, Shanté, Cindy, Tamara, Nicole, Robyn and Shakiera, all from Kayla's dance class, twirled gracefully across the stage. They were wearing their pink and red long tutus with glitter on them. Their hair were all in buns.

They all did arabesques in a line. When Kayla stood on one leg and raised her other leg, her ankle started to wobble. She slipped on the floor. She got up quickly and did a lovely arabesque with the other flowers.

I hope nobody noticed me fall, thought Kayla.

Then all the flowers started spinning around and formed a circle. They flapped their arms up and down like petals in the wind. Then they huddled together and formed a beautiful bouquet which ended the Waltz of Flowers.

Then the flowers stayed on the stage with all the other dancers in the Land of Sweets.

There's Amber, wearing her tiara, and Dylan, sitting on the throne, thought Kayla, standing next to Vicky on the stage.

The Sugar Plum Fairy and the prince danced a "pas-de-deux," a dance for two people. Amy and Dylan smiled at each other at the end of their dance.

All the dancers in the Land of Sweets waved good-bye to Marie and the prince, flying away in their sleigh.

The curtains went down and the stagehands quickly changed to the last scene in the living room of Marie's house.

When the curtains went up, Marie was sitting under the Christmas tree, holding her precious little nutcracker doll in her arms.

The curtains went down to end the scene.

"Get ready to take your bows," Madame said to the dancers backstage.

Then the curtains went up.

One by one the dancers of each dance got onstage and curtsied or bowed. The audience cheered and applauded loudly.

When Amber came onstage last and curtsied, the audience gave her a standing ovation, and shouted, "Bravo!"

Amber's father handed her a bouquet of red roses.

Amber took a deep curtsy, holding the roses.

Then all the dancers came onstage and took their final bows.

"Bravo!" yelled the audience.

The audience kept applauding until the curtains went down for the last time.

Madame clapped her hands. Everyone stood still backstage.

"This was a great performance. You all danced very well. Classes will begin again in January," smiled Madame.

After Kayla changed into her clothes and returned her costume, she found her parents and grandmother in the crowded theatre. They went into the lobby. Long tables with all kinds of desserts, cheese and crackers, fruits and drinks were on them.

"Did you see me fall. I messed up," said Kayla, taking a bite of lemon cake.

"But you got up quickly and danced beautifully. All dancers make mistakes sometimes," said her mother, taking a sip of lemonade.

"You were my favorite flower," laughed her grandma.

"You were wonderful," said her dad, taking a bite of cherry pie.

"Thank you," said Kayla. "Guess what happened?"

"What?" asked her mother.

"Vicky and I solved the case. Megan stole the tiara. We caught it on a photo on a cell phone. We got it back just in time for Amber to wear it," said Kayla, tears rolling down her face.

"Why did Megan steal it?" asked her mother.

"She's very jealous. It's all very confusing. I'll tell you all about it later," said Kayla.

"You and Vicky are good detectives," said her grandma.

"You're very clever. I'm proud of you!" exclaimed Kayla's dad.

"Thanks, Dad," said Kayla.

"What are you doing tomorrow night for New Year's Eve?" asked her dad.

"Mom, Grandma and I are going to watch the ball go down at midnight at Times Square on TV," said Kayla.

Her dad smiled. "That's nice. I have a long drive back to East Highland. Kayla, I'll see you soon. Good-bye," he said, hugging Kayla, her mom, and Grandma. He headed toward the exit of the theatre.

Then Vicky walked over to Kayla. "Hi," she said.

"Hi," Kayla said.

Just then, Tamara, Shakiera, Amy, Cindy, Robyn, Nicole, Julien and Dylan came over to Kayla and Vicky.

"We heard what happened. Both of you proved to be great detectives," Dylan said.

"You saved the day. You found Amber's tiara!" Cindy told Vicky and Kayla.

They all nodded and smiled.

"Thank you," said Vicky and Kayla, smiling at them.

"Good-bye," they said. Then Vicky and all of them walked away.

"The students in your ballet class are impressed with you and Vicky!" said Kayla's mom.

Grandma nodded, "Oh, yes."

"By the way, how does your ankle feel?" asked her mom.

"It only hurt a little during my performance, but I was still able to dance well," Kayla said.

"I think we better go now," said her mom, and they headed to the parking lot.

When Kayla got home, she ate rice pudding with whipped cream that her grandma made and drank a glass of skim milk.

She went upstairs to her bedroom and turned on her computer. She decided to type an email to Amanda.

To: Amanda
From: Kayla

Subject: Tiara Mystery

Date: December 30

You won't believe it! Vicky and I solved the mystery! It was Megan who stole the tiara. We even got it back for Amber to wear it at the Nutcracker tonight.

Have a groovy New Year!

Kayla

Then she pressed the send button.

I'm so tired, she thought, climbing into bed. Oliver curled up at the bottom of the bed.

Chapter Twenty-Five

GIFT OF PINK SATIN

The day after New Year's Day, Kayla headed over to the school cafeteria at lunchtime. After she put a tuna fish sandwich, fruit cocktail and chocolate milk on her tray, she looked around the room for her friends.

"We're over here," called out Marissa.

She sat down at a long table where Marissa, Sarah, Crystal and Breanna were sitting on a long bench. Jamal, Tyrone, Jason, Andrew, and Matthew sat down at their table.

Jason sat next to Kayla.

"Happy New Year! It's January 2nd," said Jamal.

"Happy New Year!" echoed the girls.

"Did you all have a good vacation?" asked Crystal.

They nodded their heads. "Yes," they said together.

"We went to Florida to visit my grandparents, and I got to see my cousins," said Jamal.

"How did the ballet go?" asked Marissa.

"Really nice, but you won't believe it. Vicky and I solved the mystery," blurted out Kayla.

All their eyes were glued on Kayla's face.

"Who did it?" asked Matthew, taking a bite of his egg salad sandwich.

Kayla told them how she and Vicky were able to prove that Megan stole the tiara. She also explained how they found the tiara.

"What Megan did is really bad," said Matthew.

"Yeah, she's some sore loser," said Tyrone.

"Hey, you won the bet. Amber got to wear her tiara at the Nutcracker. Breanna and I will treat you at the ice cream parlor," said Sarah.

"That will be fun," said Kayla with a smile.

"I'll be going to the ice cream parlor with you," smiled Marissa.

"Don't forget that if the Leopards get into the playoffs, you'll take Sarah and me to the Icy Palace," said Breanna.

Kayla nodded. "Of course I will."

"You and Vicky did good detective work," said Jamal.

"Yeah, you're awesome!" said Jason.

"Thank you," said Kayla, blushing. Kayla and Jason smiled at each other.

"You're a **ballerina detective**!" exclaimed Marissa.

Kayla grinned. "That's cool."

"Would all of you like to go to the movies the week after next on Saturday?" asked Tyrone.

"Yes," they called out.

"Oh look, it's snowing outside. We can't go outside for recess," said Crystal.

They emptied their trays in the big garbage cans and headed to the auditorium to watch a movie with the other seventh-graders.

Kayla was sitting in her math class copying her homework from the board.

The last bell of the day rang.

Kayla made foot prints in the snow as she walked home.

When she finished her dinner, she did her homework. Then she turned on her computer and opened her email box. *Oh, I got an email from Amanda*, thought Kayla, reading it.

To: Kayla
From: Amanda
Date: January 1st
Hey Kayla, I'm glad you solved the mystery. You and Vicky are awesome. My class is putting on a play. I hope I get a good part. Happy Zany New Year. Write soon.
Amanda

Kayla typed a message back to Amanda.

To: Amanda
From: Kayla
Date: January 2nd
Hi Amanda,
Good luck in your play. Here's to an Exciting New Year. Keep writing.
Kayla

Dad sent me an email, thought Kayla.

To: Kayla
From: Your Dad
Date: January 1st
Hey, Kayla,

The ballet performance was super. How would you and Amanda like to go skiing again on your Feb. vacation? Call or send me an email when you can. Have a Happy New Year.

Love, Dad

Kayla hit the reply button.

To: Dad
From: Kayla
Date: January 2nd
Hiya, Dad,

Yes, Amanda and I want to go skiing with You for my Feb. break. Cheers to the New Year!

Love, Kayla

Oliver suddenly scooted into the room and jumped on her lap. She patted his head and thought to herself, *I can't believe I'm going skiing again. I wonder what adventures we'll have next time.*

The next week on Thursday afternoon, Kayla was copying her homework from the board in her social studies class. It was the last period of the day in school. When the bell rang, students burst out of their classes.

Kayla got her things from her locker and put on her white jacket and dashed outside. The cold wind blew in her face as she headed for ballet school. She walked into the dressing room and went to her locker. She changed into her pink leotard, tights and ballet shoes in a dressing booth and tiptoed into the large studio.

"Hi," said Kayla, taking her place behind Vicky at the barre.

Vicky smiled. "Hi, I'm so glad you decided to come back to ballet school."

"Me, too," said Kayla.

"Oh look, Megan just came in," frowned Vicky.

"I guess Megan is going to a therapist now," whispered Kayla.

"Megan couldn't take dance lessons here anymore if she didn't go," whispered Vicky.

Madame Sofia turned on slow music on the stereo. She clapped her hands.

"Let's start our warm-up exercises with demi-pliés," called out Madame.

Then they did relevés and other exercises, holding onto the barre.

"Everyone come to the centre now," Madame said.

They practiced their arm movements and arabesques, balancing on their own.

As the music got faster, the dancers did pirouettes,

spinning and turning around the room.

"Now do leaps," Madame said.

Julien, Connor and Dylan, wearing white T-shirts, black shorts, white socks and black ballet shoes, leaped very high in the air.

"Oh, no," yelled Julien, crashing on the ground when he landed. He quickly got up.

Madame clapped her hands. "It's time to stop now."

All the students stood in front of their dance instructor.

"I want to tell you again that all of you were wonderful in the Nutcracker Ballet," said Madame.

"Madame, are we starting our toe dancing lessons today?" asked Cindy.

"Yes. At the end of every ballet class, the girls will have toe dancing lessons for about 20 minutes which will gradually get longer," Madame explained.

"Hooray," yelled out Cindy. All of the girls clapped their hands.

"Girls, did all of you bring in your toe shoes?" asked Madame.

"Yes," they called out together.

Madame smiled. "Girls, please change into your toe shoes now. Boys, you're dismissed."

The boys bowed to their teacher to show respect and say good-bye. They went to their dressing room, changed their clothes and left the ballet school.

The girls went into their dressing room.

"I'm so glad we'll be taking toe dancing lessons together," said Vicky. She sat on a bench and tied the ribbons around her ankle of her pink toe shoe.

"I wanted to give it a chance," said Kayla. "My mom surprised me and bought me these new pink satin toe shoes. They're very expensive," said Kayla.

"That's because they're made-by-hand," said Vicky.

"Hello," said Amber, coming over to them. "Guess what! I got into a full-time ballet school in Manhattan."

"That's great. We'll miss you," said Kayla.

"Will you write to us?" Vicky asked.

"Of course I will," said Amber.

"And we'll write or email you back," said Vicky.

"Oh, could both of you come to my house for dinner next week. My parents want to thank you for finding my tiara and give you the reward money," said Amber.

"We didn't expect any reward. It's not necessary," said Vicky.

"We want to give it to you. You both deserve it," said Amber.

"Thank you. I'd like to have dinner at your house," said Vicky.

Kayla smiled. "I'm coming also."

Amber grinned. "That's great!"

"Here's the diamond and the pink sapphire chip," said Kayla, handing them to Amber.

"A jeweler can glue the diamond back on the tiara. I'll

just keep the pink sapphire chip," said Amber, tiptoeing away.

Kayla put on her new toe shoes. The toes of the shoes were stiffened with layers of satin, paper and burlap and stuck together with glue.

"I don't know how to tie the ribbons on my shoes. I'm used to having elastic on them," said Kayla.

"I'll show you," said Vicky, helping her tie them.

They slowly tiptoed into the studio.

"My shoes feel so stiff," said Vicky.

"My toes feel so squished together," said Kayla.

"Girls, don't forget to put the tips of your shoes into the rosin box to avoid slipping on the wood floor," called out Madame.

"What is rosin?" asked Shanté.

"It's a white powder made of sap from fir trees," replied Madame.

When the girls finished dipping the tip of each of their toe shoes into the rosin, they went over to the barre.

"We will begin to dance on your toes by doing simple toe dancing exercises. They will strengthen your feet, ankles and legs," Madame explained.

"Madame," called out Cindy.

"What is it?" asked Madame.

"I can't tell the left shoe from the right shoe?" said Cindy.

"It's just like ballet shoes," said Madame. "There are no right or left toe shoes. You have to break them in," said Madame with a smile.

"Oh, I see!" said Cindy.

"Now, I will demonstrate how to relevé en pointe, which means in French, raised on your toes," Madame said.

Madame wore a white leotard, white tights, a short white silk skirt and her dark brown hair was in a bun. She pushed up and stood on her white satin toe shoes.

"It's your turn. Face the barre and hold onto it with both hands and look into the mirror. Now push up onto your toes and come down in a demi-plié," said Madame.

When Kayla rose up on her toes, her ankles started wobbling. She started swaying back and forth and landed on her face.

Nicole and Shanté started giggling.

I feel so embarrassed, thought Kayla.

"Girls, let's relevé on your toes again," said Madame.

As the dancers went up on their toes, Cindy bumped into Nicole and Nicole bumped into Shanté. Cindy, Nicole and Shanté slipped on the floor.

"Cindy, it's your fault," snapped Nicole.

I'm not the only one who Nicole picks on, thought Kayla.

"Relevé again," Madame said.

The girls rose up on their toes, and they all had a good landing.

"Very nice," said Madame. "Now I'm going to teach you the first part of the toe dancing exercise called échappé, which means escape in French."

Madame demonstrated it.

"Madame is such a good dancer," said Shanté.

"It's your turn. Face the barre and hold onto it with both hands. Bend your knees in fifth position. Now spring up on your toes with your legs apart. Now come down in a demi- plié," Madame commanded.

Kayla slipped on the floor. "My f f feet got stuck together," she stammered.

"Ha, ha," Nicole giggled. Megan started to laugh but put her hand over her mouth.

"It will take time for you to get used to dancing in toe shoes," said Madame soothingly. "Let's do it again," she said.

As the girls sprang up on their toes, Tamara, Shakiera, Shanté and Vicky bumped into each other. They fell on the floor. They scrambled themselves up.

All the girls started laughing.

"Dancing in toe shoes is mad hard," yelled out Shakiera.

"Yeah, my legs feel like jelly, but I still like it," said Robyn.

"Toe dancing is not easy, but it's very special," said Madame, her hazel eyes sparkling. "Now échappé again."

The girls sprang up on their toes, and they all had a smooth landing.

"You all did good work today. It's time to stop," said Madame with a grin.

The girls looked at Madame.

"I want to congratulate Amber for getting accepted into a full-time ballet school. This is her last class. I'm very proud of her," said Madame.

The girls clapped their hands.

"Thank you," said Amber, a tear rolling down her cheek. Then she curtsied to everyone.

The girls curtsied to Madame.

Then they went over to Amber and wished her good luck.

"We'll miss you," said Shakiera, Tamara and Robyn, hugging her.

Megan came over to Kayla. "Would you like to practice toe dancing with me? We can dance in my basement at my house," she said.

"Umm, alright. Maybe we'll get together some day," said Kayla. *I don't believe Megan is being so nice,* she thought.

Then Vicky and Kayla tiptoed very slowly on their toe shoes to their lockers.

"Eww, my toes hurt," moaned Kayla.

"I'm so excited. I don't care that my toes hurt and I've got a blister," laughed Vicky.

"I don't believe we danced on our toes today," remarked Kayla, munching on a red grape.

"I have an idea. Let's do a little toe dancing in the dressing room when the girls leave," said Vicky, sipping apple juice from a bottle.

"I think all the girls have left now," said Kayla, several minutes later.

Vicky and Kayla moved over to a big space away from the lockers. They faced each other and held hands. They slowly

191

rose up on their toes. They started swaying and fell backwards.

"It feels strange standing on our toes," said Vicky.

"Let's do it again," said Kayla. They held hands and stood up on their toes. They quickly landed.

"That was better. Do you want to try doing an arabesque?" asked Vicky.

"That's too hard, but I'll try it," answered Kayla.

Kayla and Vicky held hands and stood up on their toes on one leg. As they lifted up their other leg, their ankles started wobbling. They fell on top of each other on the hard cement floor. They burst out laughing.

"That was way too hard," said Vicky.

"Let's just stand on our toes," said Kayla.

"Alright. It's hard enough just standing up on our tippy toes," laughed Vicky.

They held each other's hands to steady themselves and stood way up high on the tips of their toes.

"I feel like I'm flying. I wonder what the ballet will be for our next big performance," Kayla said.

"Whatever it will be, we'll be dancing on our toes," said Vicky.

They took a deep curtsy, and giggling, swept their arms to the ground.

"I feel like a real ballerina, at last," Kayla beamed.

Kayla and Vicky faced each other. They took a deep breath. Standing on the tips of their toes, they raised their arms high up in the air.

ADVENTURE & ROMANCE!

ANOTHER EXCITING BOOK BY KAREN RAUTENBERG

Lady Lucy's Gallant Knight

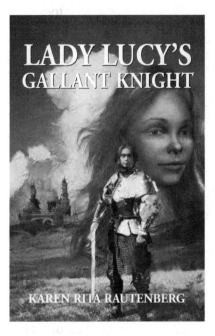

Set against the rich historical background of the Middle Ages, this tale of adventure and romance takes place in the time of serfs, lords, damsels, and knights. Lady Lucy is a headstrong thirteen-year-old, determined to marry for love no matter what tradition—or her father—dictates. When a peasant named Peter rescues her from drowning, she sets her heart on him in spite of his lowly status. But when Lady Lucy is kidnapped by an enemy of her father, Peter must prove to everyone else what lucy already believes: that his spirit is greater than his station in life and that he is worthy of her love.

DNA Press™

ISBN: 9781933255224   (1933255226)
Price: $7.95 (CAN $9.95)

Publication Date: March 2007
Publisher: DNA Press, LLC/Nartea Publishing